The Man

Who Buried Jesus

Other Books by the Same Author

Into My Own: The English Years of Robert Frost

The Bones of St. Peter

Night on Fire

Plumes in the Dust

One Day at Kitty Hawk

The Hidden Life of Emily Dickinson

Poe the Detective

Strange Harp, Strange Symphony

The Shroud

EDITOR

The Letters of Francis Thompson

John Evangelist Walsh

The Man Who Buried Jesus

A NOVEL

COLLIER BOOKS
Macmillan Publishing Company
New York

Collier Books
Macmillan Publishing Company
866 Third Avenue, New York, NY 10022
Collier Macmillan Canada, Inc.

Library of Congress Cataloging-in-Publication Data
Walsh, John Evangelist, 1927–
The man who buried Jesus:a novel/John E. Walsh.
p. cm.
ISBN 0-02-045731-6
1. Nicodemus (Biblical character)—Fiction. 2. Bible. N.T.—History of Biblical events—Fiction. I. Title.
PS3573.A4719M36 1989
813'.54—dc19 88-31166 CIP

10 9 8 7 6 5 4 3 2 1

Printed in the United States of America

For
Dot, John, Tim, Mandy, and Mat,
who were first to hear
something of this little
story—how many years ago?

Note

A passage from the personal memoirs of John, son of Zebedee:

> They both ran, but the other disciple outran Peter and reached the tomb first; and stooping to look in, he saw the linen cloths lying there, but he did not go in. Then Simon Peter came, following him, and he went into the tomb; he saw the linen cloths lying, and the napkin, which had been on his head, not lying with the linen cloths but rolled up in a place by itself.
>
> (20:4–7)

The Man
Who Buried Jesus

Part I

*O*F COURSE WE ALL KNOW that there's a reasonable explanation for the surprising, or I might better say the shocking events of the past few days. What bothers me is the utterly shameless conduct of those simple followers of his—who would have thought they had it in them to invent such a monstrous lie! If something isn't done, and quickly, they'll turn his name and his memory into an object of mockery for the whole town. Imagine all his good work ending in a wave of sneering laughter! That can't be allowed to happen.

Not that I knew him very well or very long. Hardly a year. Yet to me he was an authentic visionary, capable at times of startling penetration and insight. Yes, he was young for his role, probably still in his thirties. But there was something mellow about him, the level gaze of the dark eyes, the contained manner, so down to earth yet sort of remote. Here was a true original, the kind that appears no more than once in a generation, if that. Had he lived longer there's no telling what heights he might have reached.

Violation of sepulture is so rare and unusual a crime, I'm convinced the solution will not be found by using the same old tired methods, hauling a crowd of quivering suspects into headquarters and browbeating them. This case is more subtle than that, a job for the reasoning powers if I ever saw one, a matter of detecting small errors, a slip here, a contradiction there. How often I've said it! How often I've urged the police, theirs as well as ours, to cultivate this analytical method. Make sure of your facts, I've said to them a hundred times. Get down close to your facts and *observe.* Analyze! Look for the pieces that don't *fit.* It's like talking to a wall.

As soon as I have found the body—or can show how it was disposed of and whose hands did the deed—I'll put an end to the whole pathetic business. I'll draw up and publish a full statement of my findings, sparing no one, let guilt and punishment fall where they may. If they're allowed to get away with an insane stunt like this, who knows what might be next? It won't take long, either, for though we've barely started—not quite a week—our investigation has already uncovered several pieces of hard evidence, all tending to implicate his followers.

Of course there's still nothing that can be called decisive, not enough for an arrest.

The madness actually began a day *before* the first reports of the empty tomb reached us, on sabbath morning a week ago when an unexpected summons arrived from the Council. I was in a sourish frame of mind at the time, anyway, my sleep toward dawn having been troubled by a dream. Soundlessly it began, with the shimmering, pale green earth undulating far in the distance through billows of pearl-gray mist. Rising up slowly out of the mist there appeared an enormous, rough-hewn cross. Larger, larger, larger it loomed until at last it hung gigantically against an immense sweep of rapidly darkening sky, bolts of lightning noiselessly flashing around. Writhing on the cross like a quaking mountain there hung a body, torn, bleeding, contorted arms achingly outstretched. Suddenly a deep resounding chorus boomed forth in the silence and began reverberating endlessly across the landscape the words, father forgive them—forgive them—forgive them—forgive them. Then the gleaming blade of a prodigious spear thrust upward just as boiling masses of black clouds, rolling and tumbling in soundless wrath against the whole vast expanse of sky, enveloped the land in darkness.

Propelled awake, I rose shakily from my pillow and sat a bit dazed on the side of the bed. My anxious Sarah, roused from her own sleep by my thrashing, hovered over me as I tried to reassure her that my moans were no cause for alarm. Even when she found I wasn't ailing, she still fretted, for she firmly believes that all dreams are omens. To me they seem mostly a kind of play for the brooding mind, reflections in a mirror of a face confronting itself—doesn't Ecclesiastes tell us that bad dreams come with many cares? I've noticed, too, that there's usually a link with some event of the day before, as here.

Though it was more grotesque than most I've had, this dream didn't disturb me greatly after I was up and about, except that I couldn't throw off a somber feeling of vague uneasiness. It was enough to keep me silent at the breakfast table, not my habit by any means, which made Sarah and the two girls wonder. Making a guess at what was on my mind, Sarah tried to rouse me by bringing up something else. I can always tell when she does that.

"Nico, you really must decide about Rebecca going to Joppa. It's a whole week since they asked, and if she doesn't go, what excuse will I give? You know what your brother is like. And when is Naomi to see the new grove? She's asked several times, and Hazor says he'll be glad to come down and take her up. Isn't that nice?"

Then in an instant it came to me about the dream, those words. "Sarah! He did say that! I'd forgotten."

"What, Nico?"

"On the cross. He said father forgive them."

"Oh . . ."

"But who's *them*?"

"You didn't even hear me, Nico. I said what about Rebecca?"

"Such a thing to forget! Such a thing! Can you imagine, Sarah, how . . . What about Rebecca?"

"Nico, really, you must try and remember things. They want Rebecca in Joppa a few days for company. But you said you didn't think—"

"Yes, yes, of course she can go if she wants." Rebecca flashed that radiant smile at me which never fails to catch at my heart. "Only she must promise to dress well against the sea breeze."

"But, Nico, yesterday you said . . . oh, never mind. Now what about Naomi? Hazor says he'll bring the carriage."

"Sarah, don't you see? The man was dying, and what does he do? He says that the very people who're killing him should be forgiven!

How could a thing like that have slipped my mind?"

With that, Sarah's attention was caught by the beaming Rebecca, so involuntarily I fell to brooding again . . . how they mocked him helpless on the cross, those louts, town loafers, good-for-nothings, even some who should have known better . . . weren't nearly so quick to challenge him when he was able to answer them back . . . taunting him like unruly children, come down from the cross, save yourself, then we'll believe . . . and they laughed—how I wished at that moment that he might suddenly recover his strength, pluck out the nails and step down to the ground. How they would have shrunk back, cowering, wringing their hands! . . . What must it have been like for a dying man to have all that ugly jabber sounding in his ears? Yet he only cast his eyes slowly around on them, those patient eyes, then he lifted his face and called out, "Father," and then he paused and took a deep breath and said, "forgive them." What could he have found in that mean-spirited mob that was worthy of pardon!

"Nico? Are you listening? A meeting's been called. A messenger's here from the council."

"A meeting? But today's the sabbath."

Sarah motioned to the servant, who turned and signaled through the doorway. "Yes, sir?" said the messenger as he entered.

"What's the meeting for?"

"Dunno, sir. It's just some of the elders."

"Who called it?"

"The high priest, sir. He said only to say it was urgent and shouldn't take more than a half hour."

"All right, thank you."

A sabbath meeting was unusual, more so where no agenda was announced. Why the secrecy? Still, since immediate attendance was requested, I left the table and called for the carriage. As I went, Sarah came up reminding me about my stomach and handing me a cup of something hot. After yesterday and the restless night I'd spent, I needed no reminder. I gulped it down.

What happened next reveals just how naive I can be at times. I could also say that it shows how much wiser the elders are when it comes to the shadowy bypaths of human nature (now *there* is an admission I'm not often willing to make). When we'd all assembled in the audience room at Caiaphas' house, and the purpose of the meeting was stated, I regret to say that before I could catch myself I actually laughed out loud. One or two of the others also threw up their hands in disgust, including Joseph. Yet, as matters turned out, we were wrong. And *how* we were wrong!

Standing before us and assuming that swelled-up manner he sometimes puts on even in ordinary conversation, the high priest began by announcing that he did not trust the Galileans. Well, that hardly qualified as news. We all looked around and shrugged at one another, wondering what he was getting at. Then in a perfectly bland manner he said he was afraid that these trouble-making renegades, as he called them, might try to steal the body from the tomb, and something should be done to prevent it.

"Why on earth should they do that!" I blurted after an incredulous laugh had escaped me. From the others there also arose a murmur of puzzlement.

The high priest's accusing gray eyes and grayer beard came portentously around to where I sat in the third row. No doubt he was recalling at that moment what had happened several weeks back when all this began to unfold, the loud objection I had impulsively raised in council to the lack of a proper trial. That belated, halfhearted stand in favor of simple justice had failed miserably because I lacked the stomach to insist. Worse, it had gained for me nothing but suspicion. Caiaphas had snapped, "Are you one of them too?" deliberately making me back down and heading off further dissent. If only we could live such moments over.

Looking at me but aiming his words at all those present, the high priest asked irritably, "You recall that imposter saying what would happen after he spent three days in the grave? What is to stop those ignorant followers of his from stealing the body, hiding it away, and telling the people that he *has* risen? Even you, Nicodemus, must see that the last fraud would be worse than the first."

"Risen? From the grave?" I asked, not quite believing my ears. "You mean tell people he has come back to life? But that is preposterous! Excuse me. I mean, these Galilean rustics? Who would possibly believe them? Why should *we* be concerned if a few idiots *did* believe them?"

That any intelligent man might find reason to worry over such a thing, should call a meeting on the holy sabbath about it when to reach here some had to travel more than the allowed distance, astonished me. That Caiaphas should go so far as to soberly propose guarding the tomb of a dead man seemed pure folly. I confess I began to wonder about his mental balance. He was never the steadiest of men.

It's true that there had been some remarks made about a renewal or rising, which I suppose expressed the hope that his teachings would live on. Or perhaps it was emblematic of the afterlife—I can't deny that often he came at things in an oblique, allusive way. But to expect that his followers—these provincial fishermen!—would have the imagination, the boldness, to turn his innocent words into a prediction of *this* kind! I have met several of them, mostly in passing. They are sturdy fellows with good hearts. Though devoid of learning, they are by no means unintelligent. But beyond that, no.

As usual, Caiaphas had his way, which meant asking Pilate to assign a guard of Roman soldiers to the tomb. Pilate gave his permission, but only after some of his usual sneering—why couldn't we use the temple police, didn't we trust our own people, all said with that maddening smile. He offered us a small detachment to serve for five days, half a dozen men under a centurion. I had expected the command to go to the same Centurion Longinus who'd been in charge of the crucifixion party. Instead, another man was picked, a certain Vinucius, whom I'd heard of but never met. As we learned later, he was thoroughly disgusted at the prospect of such unsoldierly duty, and who could blame him?

By sabbath afternoon they had set up the centurion's tent, siting it on the level ground some sixty or seventy feet away from the tomb's front. The guards—armed with short swords and spears, no less!—would stand alternate watches, each pair taking the usual three hours while the others slept or relaxed. This allowed a full six hours off in the rotation for each man, not a demanding assignment. At all times the two on duty would have the tomb in sight.

Before settling down to start their cooking fire, Vinucius and his men proceeded as instructed to make a check on the body—already, one night of opportunity with the tomb unguarded had passed, a fact not overlooked by the high priest. They went to the tomb, rolled back the heavy stone, and briefly inspected the body still lying there enveloped in its shroud. Then they came out and replaced the stone.

The high priest's next move took even the guards by surprise, when a man he sent stepped up with a brisk show of authority. Across the center of the stone he strung a taut cord. With dabs of mortar he fastened the two ends of the cord to the tomb wall on either side where he'd gouged the rock a little. The cord's center he fixed to the stone's middle, also with mortar, and fastened it with gums and resins at several other points.

At sight of this, the Roman soldiers grumbled openly about not being trusted. They were right. The seal was the high priest's canny little way of letting them know that they, too, were under scrutiny when it came to matters like bribery or other professional lapses.

That evening, as I thought of the heavily guarded tomb, and him lying there in the dark chamber, I could not keep my mind from reaching back regretfully to the timid way in which I first approached him. That was just a year ago and it still pains me to recall it. Afraid of what my righteous colleagues might say behind behind my back if they knew of the visit, I actually sneaked into his house after dark! Sneaked in like a convict on the run!

Still, that wasn't the whole story, and I must be fair to myself, for Sarah too played a part in my caution. She'd ask, shouldn't we think of our position of responsibility in the community, shouldn't we think of our daughters' futures? Did I really need to go chasing after every new holy man who found his way down from the hills? I'd answer, but *this* holy man is different, and she'd come right back with her usual uh-huh, uh-huh, aren't they all. If only she could have met him, heard him talk! She's not as cynical as she makes out sometimes, and is very quick to feel these things.

Born again, he said to me the night of that first visit, every man must be born again. Of water and the spirit, as I recall. Strange idea, the way he put it, both of us sitting there at the table in the dim flicker of the small lamp between us. That which is born of flesh is flesh, he said in his strong voice, that which is born of spirit is spirit. Put me very much in mind of Ezekiel.

Something else he said that night also stuck in my mind, I'm not sure why, except that it was evocative in a poetic kind of way. It was about the wind. While we were discussing the unsearchable ways of the spirit, he brought up the wind as an example. Always it blows where it wills, he said, but you can't tell where it comes from or where it goes, and so it is with everyone who's born of the spirit. When I asked him to explain, his only reply was, "Are you a teacher in Israel, Nicodemus, and you don't understand? These are earthly things. What if I should speak of heavenly things?" He had the most unsettling way of bringing you up short with a few words.

That first meeting lasted for more than an hour, and when I left him my poor head was positively spinning from the stimulus of his talk. I lay awake half the night mulling it all over, seeing in memory that calm face with those direct eyes shining in the lamplight as they peered across the table at me. Yes, and then I recall with sorrow the awful, heartbreaking appearance of that same face only yesterday . . .

But no, I won't allow myself to dwell on that part. If I'm to keep myself to a strict line of cold analysis, then everything of an emotional nature must be excluded.

◆

IT WAS the morning after the council meeting, just about sunrise. I was in bed upstairs. There came a loud, rapid knocking at the main door, then there was a subdued flutter of women's voices, several of them and all talking at once, but in lowered tones. No doubt Sarah, thinking I was asleep, had uttered a caution. I was not asleep. I had hardly slept all night except for a wink here and there. At my age the mind doesn't clear itself so quickly.

Seconds later Sarah was at my door, knocking softly and peeking in. I said yes, I was awake, what was it?

"Joanna is here and she's very upset. She came only for a

moment. She says they were at the tomb this morning and . . ." Seeing me throw back the covers she paused, then added, "She'll tell you herself." I took my robe and we went down.

Joanna is from Galilee, but she's known to Sarah's family here in Jerusalem. In her early twenties, she's a sensible young woman not easily imposed on, and rather attractive in that fresh, upcountry way. Chusa was lucky to get her, as Sarah never tires of saying, and I agree, for she might easily have done better. She had been to our house many times, and lately had made no secret of her connection with the Galileans. In fact, on those visits she had talked of little else than her dedication to the group. Naturally this had annoyed Sarah, though she's too polite to say anything that might embarrass a guest.

Joanna stood up and looked straight at me as I entered the lamplit sitting room, her eyes wide, nervous anxiety playing over her features. She always did have an expressive face. "Oh, sir!" she burst out, coming toward me with her hand reaching. "The body is gone! It's not there! What has happened, what shall we do?"

"Gone? Who?"

"We saw the place in the tomb. The body's not there!"

"Joanna, please sit down. There, now be calm. Tell me slowly." I poured her some water but she ignored it.

"We went to the tomb this morning, you know, as we were supposed to. Early, just before sunup. It was open so we went right in, all the way. And there was nothing there. No body at all. Just empty! Who could have taken him? Why should anyone do such an awful thing?"

Her agitation, growing as she talked, was having its effect on my wife and daughters, for they stood staring at her wide-eyed, the two girls with hands to their mouths. I was less affected by her excitement, but only because the truth had dawned on me right in the middle of her breathless tale.

"Joanna, who was with you? Was Magdalene?"

"Yes. I mean no. We all started together from the house, but some of us waited to buy spices and we told Mary we'd catch up. She didn't want to stop so she went ahead."

"By herself?"

"I think so. Yes, she did. She's like that."

"And the rest of you came along a few minutes later?"

"Not long. Ten minutes."

"And did you find her there at the tomb?"

Plainly, this was the first time the thought had occurred to the girl. She looked at me quizzically a few seconds before answering. "No, we didn't, but . . ."

"Joanna, my dear girl," I said, trying not to smile too broadly, "don't you see what happened? You and your friends went to the wrong tomb!"

That suggestion stopped her for a moment; her lips parted as she was about to speak. Then she went on, spreading her hands in a gesture of insistence. "No, no, how could that be? We were all at Golgotha, watching. We saw the place where you and Joseph put him, we all knew—"

"You had very little light at that early hour, Joanna. Golgotha is scattered round with hills, bushes, trees, other tombs, all of them very much alike. Now tell me, weren't you just a bit scared to find yourself there in the cold, silent dawn? A lonely graveyard, with no one else about? You could easily have made a mistake, couldn't you? Gone to one of the newer tombs, one that hadn't been used yet, so the stone stood open?"

She glanced round uncertainly at Sarah and the girls, her smooth brow wrinkling and a shade of doubt in her eyes. Yet I could see that she wasn't convinced. "Oh, there *was* someone there," she said, turning back to me. "I forgot. A young man. He spoke, but Salome and I were behind the other women a little, so we couldn't hear. Anyway, we didn't know him."

"Where did you see this man?"

"Right at the tomb. When Salome and I got there, the others were all rushing out, and I saw him inside. Not all the way in. He was standing in the door of the vestibule. I could see his white clothes in the shadows. All white."

"You're sure nobody recognized him?"

"He was a stranger. Salome asked us while we were running off, and everyone said he was a stranger. I didn't see him too well except for the white clothes. But I could tell he had no beard. All of our men have beards."

An unidentified man wandering freely in a heavily guarded area at that hour of the morning was proof enough of the women's silly mistake. Impatience began to take hold of me, as well as some resentment that the women should have turned their solemn task into a circus of errors. I'm afraid I spoke rather brusquely. "You're sure there was no one else?"

"Yes, sir, no one."

"Joanna, since yesterday afternoon there's been a detachment of Roman soldiers guarding the site. This is true. I myself took part in the arrangements. You and the others were at home yesterday so you couldn't have known. But if you were at the right place you would have met those guards."

More important to me than Joanna's confusion was the fact that the body had been left by these scatterbrained women without proper burial. No doubt her excited companions were even then hurrying around the town spreading their news in every direction. I could only hope that the men would have the sense to see through their chatter, enough sense to ask questions.

In any case, one thing was clear. Since the women had failed in their task, I now had a personal duty to make sure that the burial rites were completed, in proper fashion and without delay. The picture of his bloodstained body lying untended in its temporary shroud, to all appearances neglected by his own friends, I found quite upsetting. There's usually a fitting and preferred way to do things in this life, especially when it comes to debts of respect and honor. Such obligations have always impressed me deeply.

Not taking time to think how she might feel about it, I turned to Sarah and said we'd go to the tomb and finish the task ourselves, all of us, including the girls. How long would she need to prepare the wrappings and the ointments and such? In anything that calls for prompt action and a level head she's usually very good, but now she just stood there with that funny look around the mouth, sort of a mild disgust. I knew what she was thinking, and I didn't like to insist—with Sarah I almost never insist—though I knew very well we couldn't do it right without her.

"Please, Sarah, after yesterday you needn't worry about me being mixed up in it. Who doesn't know by now that I helped to bury him? Please?"

Her mouth softened and her eyelids slowly descended as she let out a small sigh. Then in a resigned tone she answered, "All right, Nico," and she turned to face Naomi and Rebecca. Quietly she fired off instructions that sent each running from the room in a different direction. Then she called Joanna over and gave more orders. "We'll be ready in half an hour," she said over her shoulder as she urged Joanna ahead of her out the door.

The shortest way to Golgotha from my villa leads diagonally past the Hasmonean Palace, then along several of the narrow streets by the wall to the Yeshana Gate. It's a walk of some thirty minutes or more, and not much faster riding because of the maddening congestion on most days, milling crowds and rushing vehicles of every sort. I'm afraid Jerusalem is no longer the spacious, easygoing town it was in my youth. People then at least had time to be civil. There was none of this frenzied rushing about as if everyone's life depended on getting from here to there, never mind what they did when they got there. Now I know that's true and I don't care *what* Sarah says about me changing, because she says things like that only to annoy me when she's in one of her moods.

When we arrived at the Yeshana Gate the sun was well up and it promised to be a bright day. Joining the steady stream of people and carts noisily jostling its way in both directions we walked on through, then we turned north, skirting the moat. As I looked up the road at the strung-out parade, going and coming, men and women and children and horses and goats and donkeys and whatnot, I thought gloomily, what a funny world we live in. Were any of these very busy people giving one moment to his memory, were they thinking about him at all?

Two days, two short days! Already the tragedy of his death was forgotten, dismissed as yesterday's stale news. At that moment I felt as if I'd become an alien in the land, a stranger, cut off from familiar things. Here we had the whole world going dutifully about its business unconcerned, while I was bound on the most mournful of errands, one I had thought was finished. It would not be pleasant to look at and touch that poor, broken body a second time.

From the road as you walk toward it the low hill of Golgotha is off to the right. Its broad, rough top is visible well before you reach the vicinity, but the tomb lies around toward the far side and is pretty well screened till you're almost on top of it. After walking along the road for ten minutes or so, at a brisk pace though not so hurried as to attract attention, we came abreast of the narrow path leading between the two old cypress trees. There we turned in.

Thinking back, I recall that I first glimpsed the shadowed vestibule through a clump of trees and at an angle. When I saw that the closure stone appeared to be standing well off center my reaction was prompted more by logic than anything else. Halting abruptly in my tracks, I looked around. "That can't be the one," I said. "We took a wrong turn from the path. The tomb is farther on."

Sarah, shading her eyes from the sun and staring hard, disagreed. "No, Nico, this is Joseph's tomb. But look, it's open."

The five of us hurried forward. Pausing outside the vestibule, we all stared. The large stone had indeed been rolled entirely to one side, to the left. The low entrance into the burial chamber was uncovered, completely open, with the bright sunlight creeping into the chamber along the earthen floor.

Four quick steps carried me across the vestibule. As I bent over, reaching hastily for the sides of the low entrance, my sandal caught on the hem of my robe, and my momentum brought me stumbling to the ground. Dropping my hands before me, I crawled on through, painfully aware of the pebbly dirt grinding into the flesh of my knees.

Inside I quickly raised up, still kneeling, and turned my head to look at the niche on the right, where we had placed the shrouded body. It was empty. I could see nothing at all on the stone bench.

"Nico?" Sarah called anxiously from outside. "What is it? What do you see?"

I turned and looked at the niche in the rear wall. It was empty. I swung to the left. That niche was empty, too. I got to my feet. Stooping over the slab in the right-hand niche where we had placed the body, I ran my hand up and down the surface of the stone bench. Nothing, except for the sticky remains of the spices and what appeared to be dried blood where the head had lain.

"Nico?"

Groping backward across the chamber, I sat down on the stone slab of the niche opposite. Numbly I stared at the dirt floor. I was dumbfounded to think that, against all common sense, Caiaphas had been right. His Galilean followers, of course. Who else would have an interest in the body of this man urgent enough to risk violating a tomb? But how in the name of heaven had they managed it? Only then did I remember the Roman guards.

"Nico, it's gone!" Sarah was crouching in the doorway.

"Yes, yes, it's gone. Did you see any of the guards out there? Where are the guards? Let me pass."

Outside, I stood at the vestibule door and swept my eyes carefully around the whole area. There was no one in sight, no sound. The centurion's tent, too, was missing from under the trees. I stepped out and hurried round to the north side of the high, spreading hill. Climbing a little way up the lower slope, I stopped and looked. Not another soul in the vicinity. I cast my eyes higher. Above me at the wide summit I saw the three empty crosses still looming, lifted up stark and black against the pale blue of the sky. Hateful instruments, I thought, lifted up like that. They should already have been removed and broken up, but your professional soldier will never do that kind of job unless he's given a direct order.

Lifted up—the phrase stirred in my memory—lifted up. Where had I heard those words before? Yes, he used them the night of my visit last year—but how? Try as I might to recall it, the memory stayed tantalizingly just out of reach as I turned and walked back down the rocky slope.

Setting aside the problem of the missing guards, I asked myself where these grave-robbing Galileans could have hidden the body. Disposal of a corpse in a hurry so that it couldn't be traced would be no simple matter. They might have sneaked it into the city, of course, though the open country to the east, toward Bethany, would make more sense. Out that direction there'd be a hundred chances for a quick reburial. And he had some good friends in Bethany, those two sisters and their brother, the one whose brief illness a while back caused that weird buzz of talk.

At the tomb I found the women talking excitedly, and as I approached Joanna threw a questioning glance at me. Expecting an apology, I decided. Well, she was entitled to one.

Or was she? Where and how did the women who came to the tomb fit into all this? For that matter, had any of them actually come here? Were they all in on it with the men? Why would Joanna seek me out with a lie?

"I'm sorry I doubted you, Joanna. Can you un——"

"Oh, please don't apologize, sir. I know I must have seemed awfully foolish."

"Tell me, Joanna, I've been wondering. How did you women expect to get into the tomb? There were no men with you to move the stone. At least you mentioned none."

"Oh, that was all mixed up. We'd forgotten about it, except for Salome. We were almost here when someone remembered and said we wouldn't be able to get in. But you know there are men, the gardener and his helpers, who take care of this whole place, the tombs and the plants and trees. Salome told us she'd already sent them a message, and we'd wait till they came."

"How many women were with you?"

"There were five. Six if you count Magdalene."

"And what brought you so quickly to my house? You must have come almost straight from here."

"The others said I should."

"Where were the women going when you left them?"

"They went to tell Peter."

"What about Magdalene? You and the others didn't see her. Where do you think she went?"

"I wonder about that. Maybe she saw the empty tomb and then went back another way. She's very brave, but I'm sure she would have been as frightened as we were. And she was alone."

"The young man you saw, the stranger. Dressed in white, you say. Is that so very unusual?"

"Not just white. You know the way the moon sometimes has a glow around it? Like that. But now I'm not so sure, I mean with the darkness and the shadows and the bright torch and everything, and all of us running away so scared."

The troubled look that had gradually come over her face seemed to say that there would be little value in further questioning. In any case, there were several things I wanted to accomplish, and without more loss of time. "Joanna, you must do me a favor, if you will. Do you know where Magdalene lives?"

"Yes."

"Run and find her. Have her come to my house. Say I want to ask her about this morning. I think she'll come, but if she refuses, then tell her—in a nice way, mind you—that as an officer of the council I require her attendance." She pulled her veil tight under her chin with one hand, gathered her skirts with the other, and ran off.

To Sarah and the girls I said we would shortly be returning to the city. Meanwhile I wanted to have another look around inside the tomb. They waited in the vestibule to escape the sun, still talking.

Inside I sat down on the left-hand stone bench, opposite where the body had lain. Dumbly I looked at the earthen floor, shaking my head. The whole sorry business, I told myself, was nothing short of ridiculous, that was the only word. Absolutely it should never have happened, *could* never have happened. But it did. With my own hands I had stretched his bloody corpse in this chamber and covered it, right there in the empty niche opposite me. Now it was gone.

Had it been snatched from under the noses of the guards? Bribery didn't seem possible. In these circumstances it would be much too sensitive and dangerous. A silent attack on the two men standing watch? That too would have been a desperate move. Even with the two guards out of the way, four other guards were close at hand. Rolling back that big, heavy closure stone, no matter how carefully it was done, certainly would have created *some* noise and probably a good deal—the bumping, the scraping, the groaning, just as I'd heard it when the men rolled it shut. And in the dead of night, when this place is soundless?

A thought kept nagging at me—in some crazy way could the women themselves, alone and unaided, have been the culprits? Who can tell what excesses women are capable of in their grief? In some sudden frenzy they might have decided to take the body away instead of completing the burial, not even thinking what they would do with it afterward. But no. These women could never have budged that heavy stone. Its size and shape and position limited the number who could get near to help. Four at most, and that wouldn't have been enough. And of course there were the guards.

While these ideas went tumbling through my mind, I had been gazing down in an abstracted way at the chamber floor. Now I became aware that the light, dry soil was considerably scuffed about. In many places the shallow impressions left on it by sandals could be seen, some whole but mostly heels and toes. Many overlapped or lay broken up by the shuffling of feet. The heaviest traffic was from the middle of the chamber forward to the door.

Absently, as my mind raced on, my eyes had been tracing the curving edges of these impressions, and I found myself trying to remember something I'd read or heard about such footmarks. It was something quite clever, how they'd been used to detect lawbreakers, to expose a crime. Then it came to me, one of the Daniel stories. This old Babylonian king had a favorite god, a larger-than-life brass idol kept in a special room. Overnight the idol would devour all the food placed before it during the day, a mysterious feat that had mightily impressed the foolish old monarch. Daniel, by secretly spreading a thin layer of ashes on the marble floor, was able to expose the trick of the priests. Their footmarks gave them away. They had a hidden door by which they entered the idol's room at night.

I bent over, took off my sandals, and inspected the soles. Both were a good deal worn away at the heels, and the left heel had a ragged, circular gouge in it. The right sole had a sliver of leather torn from the outside edge, and beside it there was a thin cut. Crouching down, I began searching, and in the dirt alongside the right niche I found what I was looking for. It was an impression of my right sandal, worn heel, sliced edge and all. Farther off I found a mark of my left sandal, with the gouge in the heel rather distinct. Interesting, I thought, very interesting, especially when all the unusual features in a sole were taken together.

All told, I counted eighty-seven footmarks spread around in the chamber, partial or whole, with many overlapping. This seemed a lot, considering the number of people known to have entered. Judging by size and shape, a small portion were those of women—a welcome relief for my suspicions. Probably not more than two of Joanna's party had come in, and their immediate fright I suppose must have kept them rooted to one spot.

For the rest, disappointingly, few of the marks bore any outright distinguishing traits. I did recognize several thick, square-toed impressions as typically those of a Roman officer. This would have been Centurion Vinucius, when he came in to check on the body that first day. The only mark of real interest that I could find showed about half of a right sandal, a bit larger than ordinary, larger than mine. Neither Joseph nor my servants had especially big feet, as I recalled, so this mark intrigued me. A vague X-shaped mark could be seen near the toe, probably a repair, and a thin, shallow crack split the sole near its center.

I went to the low entrance door, called to Sarah and asked her to tear off a piece from the white linen swathing bands she had in her bag. Then I had Naomi take some of the dark ointment we'd brought and dilute it with water from the brook under the trees. Rebecca I sent to find me a pointed twig. With the piece of linen laid on top of the large sandal mark, I took the twig, dipped it into the solution, and traced an outline of the sole. Next I moved the linen to the floor beside the impression, then exactly sketched in the crack and the repair.

I stood up and was blowing on the cloth to hasten the drying, when Sarah spoke from the entrance, her voice urgent. "Nico! Nico! Magdalene is here."

Ducking through the doorway—and bumping my head hard in the process, so unsupple do the joints become with age—I saw her from the vestibule. She was approaching from the left, still forty or fifty feet away, walking quite slowly. Her usual upright carriage was sadly slumped, and long wisps of her abundant black hair straggled before her face. Eyes fixed on the ground, she didn't look up until she came near. Then as she turned into the vestibule she gave a start at finding us standing there, and her head lifted abruptly. Red eyes and glistening cheeks made it plain she'd been crying.

"Mary, thank you for coming. But I told Joanna to have you go to my house. I didn't mean to bring you out here."

"Joanna?"

"Didn't Joanna tell you I was looking for you?"

"No." Her voice sounded flat and gave off a note of dejection. I was sorry to see her face, an attractive one in that mature way, so drawn. "Tell me, Mary, why have you come back? Weren't you here this morning early?" Her reply scarcely answered my question. She seemed almost to be talking to herself.

"They wouldn't believe me when I told them the body was missing. They said I must have been at the wrong tomb. I knew I was at the right tomb. But they said I couldn't have been." Suddenly she looked straight at me. "*You* know his body is gone; you were inside. Who has taken it?" Nervously she lifted both hands to her face, wiping at her cheeks.

"Mary, exactly what happened out here this morning?"

"I came ahead of the others. The tomb was open and I saw the body was gone, so I ran back and told Peter and John. They just said I should sit down and rest. Then I went and told the others and none of them would listen either." Dropping her hands from her face, she looked up suddenly, reached out and touched my arm. "Oh, I know what they think about me, that I get too excited sometimes over little things. I know that. But you see I was right, this time I was right. He's not in there, is he? Please go and tell them. They'll believe *you*."

"You saw nothing else this morning; no guards?"

"Guards? Why should there be guards? No, there was nothing else, no one."

It was obvious that the woman was too upset to be questioned further, nor was it likely that she had much more to tell. Suggesting that in her state she shouldn't be out here alone, I invited her to return to the city with us. Shaking her head she turned away. She'd stay at the tomb a little while, she murmured, then go home and see if they'd believe her this time.

Still uneasy about her, after we'd gone a short distance toward the road I stopped and looked around. She was leaning dejectedly against one of the small pillars that flank the vestibule, head sunk down and hands clasped together at her throat. From what I could see of her face it looked as if she was weeping again. I'm afraid it's true what they say of her, I concluded, a good-hearted, intelligent woman, yet not quite steady, always liable to go overboard. Too bad really.

I was just turning around again to catch up with the others when my gaze lifted, fixing on the three dark crosses standing atop the hill. For a second I allowed my eyes to linger, thinking how curious it was that from a distance, and backed as they were by the vast expanse of blue sky, they seemed actually to have lost a good deal of their sinister aspect, that disgust and horror they conveyed when seen close up. Then, before the thought had faded, into my mind there popped that tantalizing, vagrant memory I hadn't been able to recall earlier—as Moses lifted up the serpent in the wilderness, he said to me that night in his veiled way, so must the son of man be lifted up. Those were his exact words and I heard them in memory as clearly as if it had been yesterday: Just as Moses in the wilderness lifted up the serpent, so must the son of man be lifted up.

Cryptic the saying certainly was, though of course I knew well enough what Moses did. To protect his people in the desert from the fatal bite of the fiery serpents, he had a special bronze image of a serpent made. Then he placed it on top of a huge pole, raised up high. Anyone who'd been bitten could be cured just by looking up at the shining image. Seems to have worked, too. But how all that applied in the saying, or who this son of man might be, I still couldn't tell, and once more I felt sorry I had not asked more questions that night. So many things he said during the time I knew him I wish I had the chance of talking over now. Too late, too late.

As I saw it, our first task was to determine *how* the body could have been taken from the tomb, the method used. From that information perhaps we could work our way to the identity of the perpetrators. To proceed logically, we needed to have all the circumstances prior to the crime lined up in proper sequence and setting. The odd detail, any little thing out of place, should then sooner or later disclose itself unaided, leap right out of all the confusion, giving us a starting point. As the four of us walked somberly back to town, in my mind I went rapidly over the leading events of that awful day, for me still all too vivid.

He died pretty quickly. That meant there was no need to hasten the end by breaking his legs, the nasty trick the officer did perform on the other two, expertly but still sickeningly. All afternoon I watched him struggling to shift his weight from hands to feet and then back again. Only when he was standing upright on the lower nail—to phrase it that ghastly way—was he able to get his breath. Every time he slumped down and hung by his arms the burden of his own weight prevented his lungs from filling. At last, gasping for air, he could neither raise himself nor breathe. Then his head dropped slowly forward, as if he were nodding grotesquely to the crowd, causing the long, matted hair to flop down in ragged strands.

In spite of all the horror of the cross, it is strange to think that his death in the end was mostly a matter of suffocation.

He had been hanging up there dead only about ten minutes when Joseph arrived back from town with the governor's permission to take the body. With him he brought the linen. There wasn't enough time before the start of the sabbath to finish the cleansing, the anointing, and the rest, so the linen cloth had to serve as his temporary shroud. Long and narrow, about fourteen feet by four feet, it would fold completely down over the body from the head. It was makeshift but would have to do until the sabbath had passed and the women could come out and finish the burial properly.

The body was released from the cross by the soldiers—no simple task, as I saw to my surprise—and lowered to the ground. Two of my servants picked it up at head and feet and followed us, Joseph and I, down the slope that descended the north side of the hill. As we advanced, the moody crowd of onlookers drifted slowly apart and back and I couldn't help but notice the way everyone's gaze followed the limp corpse as it went by. Even the ones who'd been hooting and jeering the loudest fell silent. Anyway, there's no doubt that most of those present knew exactly where he was buried.

The tomb, a new one recently purchased by Joseph for his own family—how little he thought, as he said later, who would be its first occupant!—lay only a couple of hundred feet distant, just down the hill and around to the side. Hewn right out of the soft limestone, it was tunneled into a big outcropping in the eastern foot of Golgotha Hill, a neat job of using the natural lie of the ground. About the usual size, it's much like all the other rock tombs in the area, with only the two small columns and a shallow pediment for exterior decoration.

When we reached the vestibule my two men carefully put the body down on a strip of matting and prepared to maneuver it into the chamber.

The vestibule itself is not large, only about ten feet wide and about six deep. At the rear, a small doorway is cut through the rock, leading into the tomb proper. This consists of a room ten or a dozen feet square, with space for three bodies let into the walls. Each of the two side walls, as well as the back, contains a broad, high-arched niche that is several feet deep. On stone benches within these niches the shrouded bodies are laid, one to a niche, later to be walled up with brick and mortar. The ceiling of the chamber is not high, only about seven feet. The floor is the original earth, tamped down and reasonably dry.

Between vestibule and chamber the doorway is very low, not much more than four feet high by about three broad. This is more sensible than it seems, for if it were of normal height it would need a closure stone much too big and cumbersome to move without special gear. But the stone is still formidable. Perfectly rounded, it looks like an oversize millwheel, lacking only the center hole. It's easily a foot thick and stands as high as a man. My guess is that it weighs well over a thousand pounds. Sitting in its groove it fairly hugs the chamber wall, entirely shutting off the low entrance.

Waiting in the vestibule were the two large jars of spices I had sent ahead, a prepared mixture of myrrh and aloes made up with olive oil. These a servant took inside one at a time. The body could not be carried in, of course, so the strip of matting, bearing the corpse, was pulled through into the burial chamber. We moved as gently as we could, but some of the fine grayish dust was raised, and it annoyed me to see it drifting down on the bruised flesh.

Inside, the yellowish glare of a small torch held up by the servant threw our distended shadows grotesquely on the walls. In the niche to the right of the entrance (I don't recall why we chose that one, and I can't see that the location of the body in the chamber played any role later), we spread a thin layer of the spice mixture along the top of the stone bench. Then we neatly stretched out one half of the long linen cloth, leaving the other half rolled up at the head. Some more of the spices we distributed along the length of the cloth.

The servant reached for the shoulders while I grasped the legs, and we lifted the body, placing it lengthwise on the bench atop the linen, feet toward the entrance. The wrists I picked up and crossed over the stomach, then tied them together with short strips of cloth. At the same time, Joseph bound up the bearded jaws with another strip of cloth, passing it under the chin and tying it over the top of the head.

As the fragrant spices perfumed the air around us—I was conscious of the powerful myrrh, especially—the lines of that old psalm ran through my mind, the one that had prompted me to provide these spices in such abundance. *God has anointed you with the oil of gladness above your fellows; your robes are all fragrant with myrrh and aloes,* ran two of its lines. Of course the psalmist didn't mean burial robes. But I had decided that he would have at least some of the ceremonial honor he'd been denied in life. How little it was.

The usual coins were laid on the eyes. I should say that both Joseph and I had forgotten about the coins so we had to borrow them from my servant. He had only some of those badly stamped ones recently turned out by Pilate's mint, the issue bearing an astrologer's staff and the name of Tiberius. Fitting, very fitting, I thought ruefully as I placed a circlet of imperial bronze on each of the closed eyelids.

Before rolling the top half of the linen down over the front of the body I paused for one last look to fix his image in my memory.

The face was sort of long, more square than oval, with strong and graceful brows. In life, as I well recalled, that face had shown balance and self-control, with a certain air of high intelligence, perhaps including a touch of the patrician. No, patrician wasn't right, for that implied aloofness. It was more like confidence, a natural self-reliance, or even better, an authority.

But now!

In the steady yellow glow of the torch I could see that the long chestnut hair on either side of the face was stiff with sweat and blood. The left eyelid and the brow just above it were red and swollen, as was the bridge of the nose, also the right cheek—these injuries formed a distinct welt down across the face and had evidently been inflicted by a single sharp, whipping-type blow from one of the soldier's reeds.

Blood spattered the cheeks, the mustache, and the beard, and from the scalp wounds several thicker, brighter drops had trickled down over the forehead. The broad chest was bloody too, as were the wrists and forearms. Both thighs showed many small, red bruises where the whips had cut the skin—awful sight! I think there isn't a more terrible instrument of casual torture than the Roman flagrum with its wicked metal tips.

Quickly I rolled the upper half of the linen down over the body, stretching it to meet the bottom end, which I folded back up over the feet. Along the sides I tucked in the edges while Joseph distributed the remainder of the spices. At waist and ankles I bound the cloth loosely with thin cords, not tight, just enough to keep it in place. No need to secure it more than that since the women were to arrive early the morning after the sabbath and too many bindings would only complicate their task.

Finished, Joseph and I stood there a moment, our eyes taking in the full length of the shrouded form. I noted how the pliant linen draped over his face, sloped down to touch the chest, and outlined the two converging arms. Until that instant I think I had not been fully aware of the awful extent of the tragedy that confronted us, it had all happened so fast. Now there was no escaping the stark fact, for there he lay, expressive hands unmoving, agile tongue mute, limbs already stiffening. The final touch of agony was added to the picture by the way his left knee had somehow been wrenched a bit inward, slightly lifting the cloth and distorting the line of the leg and foot.

We left the chamber and waited in the vestibule entrance for the two servants to close up by setting the stone in place.

Moving that heavy stone is no easy task, though the shallow

groove along the ground helps, since it declines a bit as it runs toward the right. The stone, in closing, thus rolls somewhat downhill. But that means, of course, that to open it again the stone has to be rolled back uphill a little, along the rising groove. While this calls for greater effort, the stone need be moved at most four feet to fully expose the entrance. Three capable men, I'm told, perhaps two, can usually manage it.

Straining at the stone, the two servants, who were both big men, rolled it slowly down into place, completely blocking the low doorway. As it moved, rubbing and scraping roughly along the tomb wall and in the groove, it gave off a loud rumbling, grating sound, almost as if it were groaning and gasping. I shuddered to hear it.

◆

THE HEADQUARTERS of the Roman cohort in the Antonia fortress is not on the direct line from Golgotha to my villa, and I didn't want to have Sarah and the girls needlessly trailing all over town after me. We entered by the Yeshana Gate, and after we walked together to the temple corner I suggested that they should go home. Someone might come to the villa looking for me with information, I said. They left, and I turned north for the Antonia, anxious to hear the centurion's explanation of the night's events.

The Roman soldiers stationed inside the city walls are a rough bunch, and it's never pleasant to go among them in the bare, stone halls of the Antonia. I'd been there once or twice before, not by choice but on council business, and I had not enjoyed it. This time was no improvement. The man on duty at the desk didn't even bother to look up when I asked if Centurion Vinucius was available, just motioned toward a small side room. "Wait in there," he directed curtly, then called a messenger over and dispatched him up the stairs.

The narrow side room was every bit as dreary as the outer hall. For furniture there was only a long, heavy table down the center, with half a dozen stiff-backed chairs set around it. The stark, white walls held only a large frescoe of Tiberius, directly opposite the door. It was a picture of himself which that gentleman would not have been flattered to see—the Roman sense of art, I've always felt, deteriorates badly the farther it gets from the capital. In this picture, I decided, Tiberius appeared not like master of the world, but like some coarse wagoneer after a night on the town (maybe true enough, in its way).

At the sound of the opening door I turned to look, and had my first glimpse of Vinucius. The sight was not promising.

Encountering one of these Roman officers in ordinary street clothes always throws me a little off stride. Without the gleaming chestplate, the crested helmet, and the swirling cape, they actually seem made of mortal flesh, almost as frail as the rest of us. When Vinucius swept in he was wearing a dark, belted, knee-length tunic of some rich material, with crimson border and half-sleeves. On his left hip conspicuously swung a large pearl-handled dagger. Though he appeared every inch the professional, he did seem young for his rank, I'd guess his late twenties. Still, the experienced campaigner showed in the angular face and the cold, blue eyes.

This one, I told myself, will require nice handling.

"Centurion Vinucius, I apologize for bothering you. I know you're busy. But it's important that I have some explanation of what took place last night at the Golgotha tomb your men were guarding. They are not there now, and the body has been taken."

In silence, his eyes studying the floor, he walked slowly to the far end of the table, pulled out a chair, placed it just so, and sat down. Then he allowed several moments to pass before looking up and answering in a loud, metallic voice. "My report's already been made verbally to the proper authorities, including your high priest. Written report to follow, copy for the archives, copy for the city council. Isn't that sufficient? Well, since you've taken the trouble to come here . . . understand, I have only a minute. Troop discipline can't be taught by an officer who ignores the day's training schedule."

He put his bare, muscular arms on the table, clasped his large hands in front of him, and looked at me straight and unblinking. "The incident is unfortunate. But these things happen. At the change of watch this morning, just before first light, the two men on duty at the tomb were found asleep by their replacements. The tomb stood open. The body was gone. The theft had been accomplished in the dark while my two men slept. That is all."

A crisp recital, to the point, offering no hint of apology, all very much in character. I wasn't sure he would sit still for any close questioning, but I had to try. "May I ask what you did when you discovered the crime?"

"Made a search of the whole area, of course. We could find nothing. The job was well planned."

"Well planned? Pardon, but I don't follow. How could the thieves plan on finding your men asleep?"

"Hadn't, of course. Came prepared to make some kind of silent attack, I'm sure. Found the guards asleep and saw there was no need to take the risk. While some of them removed the body, others must've stood over my sleeping men with swords ready. Well planned, I mean, for getting the body out and away undetected. A fast operation, well executed. Have to admire that."

"Where were your two men sleeping when they were found at the change of watch? Together just outside the tomb, at its front, off to the side?"

"Not sure that's any of your business . . . well, they had separated. One was part way up the hill, above and behind the tomb. The other lay under a bush at the foot of the hill, off to the right of the tomb. Had an agreement between them for a nap. From those positions, they thought that any disturbance would be bound to alert at least one of them."

"May I ask the names of these two men?"

"No."

"No?"

"No."

"Will I be able to speak to them?"

"No."

"Then perhaps one of our police officials . . ."

"No."

The direct stare had become positively frigid, with the grim lips set and the squarish chin thrust forward, almost as a challenge. He was my junior by about thirty years, yet I admit I began to feel acutely uncomfortable. It's amazing how Roman officers of the line all seem to have this trick of intimidation.

"But Centurion, I suppose I may assume that these two men will be properly punished?" The punishment didn't really matter to me. I put the question that way only as a means of getting past Vinucius' stiffening attitude.

"That's a Roman affair," he shot back, his voice rising, "solely in the discretion of this command! Your council's not concerned! The guards were given to you as an accommodation." He paused to regain his control, then, calmer, he went on. "However, I can tell you that there'll be no punishment of those men except for restriction to barracks."

"But surely . . ."

"My inquiry shows that no punishment is warranted, and under army regulations that's sufficient unless the governor steps in which he hasn't and won't. As a courtesy, I'll tell you that my two men were incorrectly assigned to the post in the first place. For three nights before, they'd served with the crowd control unit at the temple because of *your* feast. In that time they had little sleep, and almost none the previous night when my fool of an orderly made up the duty roster for the tomb. I knew nothing of this, and my men are not grumblers."

He shoved his chair back from the table, rose to his feet and came toward me. "You will find all this along with further details in my written report."

"But Centurion," I said, standing up as he pushed past, "what is to be done? How shall we identify those responsible? Is no search to be made for the body?"

"No question about the perpetrators," he said, stopping and looking back at me. "I thought you knew. That gang of Galileans. The man's followers."

"Well, yes, but how can you be sure, what evidence—"

"Three of the gang were seen loitering in the vicinity on the evening we set up watch. I learned this later from the guard who warned them off the premises."

"Now that's important. Who were they?"

"We have no names. The guard said he recognized them, that's all, especially one big, brawny fellow he'd seen a couple of times. I'm late."

"But the search?"

"The whole matter has been turned over to Security. That's not my department." He moved briskly toward the door.

"Oh, Centurion, one moment if you please. One question, a small thing. But allow me to ask it."

He halted, swung partly around and leveled a look of fierce impatience that might have stopped me. But this was something that disturbed my sense of fitness. "Considering the hour at which the theft took place, I assume that you were in your tent sleeping, and that the other off-duty guards were asleep nearby. How do you think the Galileans were able to roll back that big stone without waking at least some of you with the noise?"

He stared at me for a moment as if surprised by the question. Then he snapped a curt "There are ways," and strode out, leaving the door open.

Yes, I suppose there are, I thought. So why run off instead of talking about them? Never mind. When I reach home I'll have just the man to help get me an answer. But first I had more pressing business.

◆

EVEN IF I COULD find the house would Peter be there? I had no idea. But a meeting with this man, the most interesting of the Galileans, calmly face-to-face, was uppermost in my mind as I walked quickly down the Antonia's broad steps.

I had spoken with Peter only twice, briefly, yet I'd been much taken by his easy, smiling manner. The only thing I didn't like about him wasn't his fault, that heavy Galilean accent. The guttural slurring grates on me, and with Peter's forceful manner it's even more pronounced. He's a natural-born talker, full of homey stories about his life as a fisherman. But rough and ready as he is, he's fluent and quite confident of himself. Fairly intelligent, too, the broad, intuitive sort you sometimes find among the uncultivated.

Physically he's impressive, just about the most powerful-looking man I've ever met—"big, brawny fellow" is a fair description. He's my own height, an inch or two above average. But his frame is broad and remarkably deep through the chest. The massive shoulders and arms really seem capable of lifting a horse. Yet he's not brutish. His head, with its curly black hair and beard, is well shaped, and he moves with that peculiar ponderous grace you see where great muscular strength is under control.

I turned into the main street and joined the crowds streaming past the temple. As I did so I found myself thinking that Peter might be able to roll back a sepulcher stone all by himself.

A few minutes of brisk walking and I had put the Hasmonean Palace behind me, along with most of the crowds, and had plunged into the maze of narrow streets honeycombing the city's southwest quarter.

I'd never asked where Peter and the others lived when they were in Jerusalem, and now it had occurred to me, why not that same house where my meeting with Jesus took place the year before? As I recalled, it served as a sort of central gathering place for them, a kind of headquarters. At least that was the only possibility I could think of then, and waiting to have him traced would lose precious time. Three hours had already passed since Joanna first came to me, even more than that since the body was taken.

As I understood it, the house belonged to one of the group's local members. In fact, it was the young son of the place, a boy of about twelve named Mark, who had come to my villa that night to fetch me there. We had walked in the dark, though, and I was never well acquainted with that section of town. I did recall that the place was due east of my villa and fronted on a twisty, narrow street. It had a small courtyard in front enclosed by a high brick wall with a wooden, two-doored gate in its center. The building was on the large side, and had two full floors, the upper one a single spacious room or hall that they let out for weddings and banquets and such. That night, a charming young servant girl named Rhoda carrying a lamp had answered Mark's summons at the gate.

All I had to do was find the brick wall with its double door, and to do it I was prepared for an hour's hunt through the streets. Luckily, it took only half that long. As soon as I spotted the large twin fountains attached back-to-back in the cramped square I remembered them. The house was only around the corner and down a couple of blocks toward the city wall. A few minutes later I was standing at the gate jangling the bellpull.

The smaller entry portal to the left was opened and there stood the same smiling Rhoda. Yes, she remembered me, she said, and yes, Peter was there. They were all there.

I told her I'd like to see Peter alone and she turned and led the way across the courtyard. We went into the house through a side door, walked along a narrow hallway, then came to a small, comfortable sitting room. There she left me, politely closing the door, and I could hear her scurrying off down the hall. A few minutes passed and then I heard returning steps, and the door swung open. Behind Rhoda, filling up the whole doorway, loomed Peter. Against his red-robed bulk the young servant looked like a five-year-old.

Stepping around the girl he came swiftly toward me and planted both huge hands on my shoulders. Staring hard into my eyes, he said, "You've heard?"

Apprehensively I thought, heard what?

"You mean that his body is missing? Yes." I searched the forthright face, the large intense eyes, for some sign that the broad brow concealed guilty knowledge. I saw only honest concern. But how had he come to know, or rather to believe, that the body was gone? Magdalene claimed that he'd ignored her.

"Peter, this is a very serious matter. You can tell me nothing?"

Impatiently he threw his hands wide in a gesture of annoyance as he walked to a small table at the room's center. "Nicodemus, we *know* nothing. I wish to heaven we did!"

I told myself: don't waste time, go straight to the point, take him by surprise. "I was speaking to Magdalene, Peter. She says that when she discovered the tomb empty, she ran back here and told you. She says you didn't believe her, that none of you believed her. She says you refused to do anything."

"Yes, that's true. She was upset, talking wildly. We thought that there'd been a mistake, the wrong tomb, something like that, and then——"

"Excuse me, Peter. But if you don't mind I'd like to have a look at your right sandal?"

"What?"

"Your right sandal. Would you take it off and let me have a look at it?"

"My sandal?" He looked down, then glanced back up at me, frowning. "What do you . . ."

"I have a reason. Please?"

He lifted his knee, reached down, unhooked the sandal, and handed it to me. I placed it sole-up on the table, then took from my pocket the square piece of linen and spread it beside the sandal. The footmarks in the chamber had been made by Peter, all right. The marks were identical.

Pointing to the linen, I explained, "This pattern was traced by me from a footmark I found on the floor of the tomb this morning. It came from your sandal, as you can see." I turned and faced him squarely. "You *were* at the tomb. Inside. What were you doing there? Why did you say you didn't believe Magdalene?"

He put his hands on the table and bent over, studying linen and sandal. Finally, without looking up, he said, "This is very clever. That's my sandal, all right."

Straightening, he turned to look at me while the hint of a smile played round his lips. "When you interrupted me I was about to say that after Magdalene left here, John and I were talking, feeling sorry for her. She does tend to be excitable. Then Salome and her friends came rushing in babbling the same wild story, all hurry and confusion. An angel, they said, had told them that Jesus was alive, an angel, no less. At least I think they said an angel. You can imagine how that pained us, to hear such talk. Well, it began to seem that *something* was wrong at the tomb, and then it struck me—Caiaphas! That vindictive old devil was up to something nasty, I was sure of it. I got so worked up that I took John and we went to the tomb running all the way."

"So you did go to the tomb this morning?"

"I just told you I did." There was an edge to his voice, and his eyes narrowed slightly.

"And you and John went inside?"

"It's a long run from here. I'm not built for speed, so I told John to go ahead. He was waiting for me in the vestibule. Looked a bit shaken and said that I should enter first. He's like that, you know, unusual for a young man these days. Well, as soon as we went in we saw that the body was gone. No sign of it. We were stunned, mystified, angry, horrified, whatever you like. Finally left the tomb and came back here, thinking all sorts of things, and since then we haven't stopped trying to find an answer. But how? Where do you start? I'll have my sandal now."

His story sounded plausible, with that little touch about John so casually thrown in. But what would he have said had he not been faced with that footmark? These country people learn cunning from the cradle, and I had given him too much time to think. I should have held the footmark back longer, till he'd committed himself. How cagy he'd been in his replies!

If he was telling the truth, the two must have been at the tomb only a short time before my own arrival. If he was lying, they could have been there anytime during the night.

"Sit down," Peter said, taking a chair himself off to the side. "You seem tired. And puzzled. What are you getting at, anyway?"

I sat down at the table and turned to face him. Carefully I explained about the detachment of Roman guards that had been placed at the tomb. I felt sure he couldn't have known about the guards, otherwise the women would have known. Then very deliberately I quoted Caiaphas' reason for taking the unusual action: "You Galileans would not hesitate to steal the body and go around proclaiming that Jesus had risen alive from the grave."

Peter's thick eyebrows lifted and he seemed honestly amazed. But he made no reply, only sat there staring at me. Hoping to ease him into some kind of admission, I went on. "Stranger things than that have happened. Men get carried away, caught up against their wills in something beyond them. Please, Peter, if you know anything at all, now is the time to speak. Don't let it go any further."

A shade of anger clouded his features and he waited a moment before speaking, but all he said was, "You must take us for half-wits." The dry tone of his vibrant voice managed to convey both sarcasm and disappointment.

"The body is *gone*, Peter, and you'll agree that it must have been taken by *someone*!"

He leaned forward in his chair, planting his elbows on his knees. The movement brought his large shoulders into prominence. "What of the guards? Have you talked to them?"

"The centurion admits that his men were asleep on duty. He says the body was taken just before the fourth watch came on, not long before dawn. They're quite sure that you . . . that your men did it."

"Why haven't they come after us? We haven't been hiding. Been right here all day in the house."

"Bureaucracy, of course. The case had been turned over to another department. You're in danger, all of you. I hope you realize that."

"If so, we'll deal with it when it reaches us. But I can't believe you're serious. This is sheer nonsense."

"Tell me, Peter, what do you think happened?"

He shook his head in puzzlement and tightened his lips before replying. "I honestly don't know, except for Caiaphas, somehow. It's nonsense to think that anyone could have fooled those Roman soldiers. I don't believe they were asleep. You accept things too easily. Probably they were all in on it—Caiaphas, and who knows who else, and the guards. Some cash from the temple treasury no doubt also played its part."

He paused and sighed deeply, slumping down in his chair. His attitude, judging by the look on his face, was one of utter frustration, if not of outright despair. "Nicodemus, I may not show it—someone has to hold things together—but I'm more shocked at all this than you are. All of us here want to do something, but what? In heaven's name, what? I've never had to search for a corpse before."

The door to the room swung open and the maid Rhoda stepped in. "Excuse me, Peter. I'm going to do the wash. Do you have anything?" He lifted one large hand and waved the girl away with an impatient "No, no." As she turned to leave I glanced idly at the cloth hanging in long folds over her right arm. Then she was gone, closing the door and leaving behind her a faint, pleasant aroma that hung in the air.

"Peter, if Caiaphas took the body, why in secret? And the centurion, would he agree to put blame on his own men for dereliction of duty? They could have found an easier way to do . . . whatever it was they were doing. I can't picture *that* centurion getting involved in a lie that would reflect badly on him."

Staring at the floor with his arms folded, Peter grunted one word: "Gold."

"No, the whole thing is senseless, unless there's a good deal more to it, something in the background. First Caiaphas takes the trouble to put a guard at the tomb, then he turns around and bribes those same guards to conspire with him? I can't see that."

He rubbed a large, rough hand wearily across his eyes. "You know, Nicodemus, I believed he was the Christ. Truly believed it. He asked us about that one day, asked point-blank who we thought he was. It was the same question I'd been asking myself, over and over. But *then* I was certain. I answered so fast the others had no chance to speak. You're the Christ, I said, the Son of the living God. I said exactly that to him—"

"Yes, that's interesting, and I'd like to hear more about it someday. Now, if you don't mind, let's get back to what has happened." I didn't care much for the direction his thoughts were taking.

". . . Son of the living God. I can't recall that such an idea had ever been in my mind until that instant. But no sooner had I said it than I felt a profound sense of the most pervading certainty and truth—in my heart, in my mind, glowing in every limb and portion of my body. It was like a mystical fire that consumes but does not destroy. It was a light like the sun in mid-heaven on the brightest day, warming everything, inescapable."

He was talking rapidly now, in a low, urgent tone, his eyes alight with feeling. As he spoke his right hand lifted and the long, thick fingers curled until, as he finished, his hand was a huge, tight fist. Leaning forward in his chair, his right fist raised and his left hand planted on his knee, his rugged face thrust at me, he was the very picture of strength and conviction. I had never imagined him like this, so intense, but it was not a mood that I cared to encourage, not when I recalled what Caiaphas had said. But he wasn't ready to stop.

"You know what he said to me then? Blessed are you, Simon bar-Jonah, he said, for flesh and blood has not revealed this to you, but my Father who is in heaven. Don't you see? I called him the Son of God, the Messiah, and what did he do? He accepted the title! *Accepted it.* My Father who is in heaven, he said . . . and yet, what does it all matter? So many things were said in those three years that I still don't under——"

A sudden jumble of running feet sounded in the long hallway outside the door, and there arose an excited scattering of voices, men's and women's, all speaking at once. Then, booming above the rest, a man's voice ordered, "Mary, wait! We'll call him for you. Someone's in there."

The door flung open and in rushed Mary Magdalene, wide-eyed, hair flying, and close behind her there hurried a small crowd of five or six people. Without stopping she threw a quick glance around and spotted Peter. Hands reaching for the arm of his chair, she fell to her knees beside him. Her expressive eyes were bright with brimming tears, but they were not tears of sorrow for there was such joy mirrored on her face as I have seldom seen. The others pushed close around the two, all noisily talking at once. I recognized some of them—Joanna, the boy Mark, Peter's brother Andrew, young John.

"Peter, oh, Peter," Magdalene sobbed brokenly, "he's alive! He spoke to me, I touched him! He's alive!"

Abruptly, the babble of talk ceased. All eyes sought Peter's face, waiting expectantly. Glancing over at Andrew, he asked rather sternly, "What happened? Where was she?"

"At the tomb. She ran in a few minutes ago and started talking like this."

"I saw him, spoke to him!" Magdalene went on breathlessly. "Oh, you must believe me, you must! Listen, Peter, I'll tell you very calmly."

She stopped talking, carefully wiped her eyes and cheeks with her hand and moved closer to the arm of Peter's chair. Making an obvious effort to calm herself, she took a slow breath, then went on: "I was standing in the vestibule . . ." She stopped again, looked over at me and pointed. "He was there, he saw me. A little while after he left, I heard a noise and I stooped down and looked inside. There were two men. They were sitting where his body had lain, one at the head and one at the feet. They were dressed all in white and they asked me why I was weeping and I said because someone had taken his body away. I didn't know who the men were but I didn't care and I wasn't afraid." She paused, shut her eyes a moment, then opened them and looked straight up at Peter. Now her words came rapidly tumbling over one another: "Then I turned to go and there was another man standing there outside the tomb and my eyes were full of tears that made everything a blur and my head was down and I started to walk around the man and I heard him call my name and I looked and I saw that it was him! It was the Lord!"

I have seldom been so disgusted as I was on hearing this pathetic outburst from the overwrought woman. A sharp reprimand from Peter, I thought, would bring her to her senses quickly enough. She didn't give him the chance. "And Peter, he gave me a message for you, for everyone. He said to tell you—I don't understand it, but he said to tell you—'I am ascending to my Father and your Father, to my God and your God.' Oh, John—Andrew—he's alive!"

Peter reached out and took her shining, tear-stained face gently between his big, strong hands. "Mary, hush," he said in a soft, confiding tone, "listen to me. No, be quiet now and listen. You say he's alive. Mary, Mary, we know that. We've known it all along. Yes, he's alive, and he will—"

"Peter!" I interrupted angrily, "I won't have this! Stop it! You've gone too far!"

He paused only long enough to half throw an annoyed glance in my direction, then returned his attention to Magdalene. ". . . will never die. He lives now as surely as his words live in our hearts, as surely as we love his memory and teach his truth. Of course he spoke to you, Mary. He speaks to all of us when we remember those long nights listening—"

"No, no, no!" Magdalene's voice was almost a moan. "Not like that, Peter, not like that! He's really alive, like you or me. Just as he was before. Oh, I know he died, we saw him die, saw him wrapped in a shroud in the tomb. But now he's come back from the grave, come back to us. He has, Peter, he has!"

Wrapped in a shroud? Of course, the scent! That's what I'd been trying to remember. I jumped up from my chair, went over to Joanna and took her by the shoulder. "Joanna, where is the washing done in this house? Take me there. Quickly. No questions."

She frowned and looked puzzled. Then she swung away from the little group and beckoned me toward the door. In the hallway we turned left, went along for a short distance, then turned right through another door, went down a few steps and entered the kitchen. At the rear wall she pulled open a door leading outside. "There. The shed."

Rapidly I crossed the yard and threw open the shed door. In the far corner Rhoda was standing at a table folding garments. "Rhoda, where is that long cloth you had on your arm before, when you came into the room?"

"Why, sir, it's . . ." She looked across to where a large mound of clothing lay heaped on the floor. "It's there. I was just waiting for the pot of water to heat up so I could boil it. I'm sorry. I'd have done it faster if . . ."

I started looking through the bundle, then spotted the thick, four-foot-wide roll lying half covered on the floor. I picked it up and grasped the loose edge. The rest of the roll dropped open, and I stepped back a few paces to unroll it further. Immediately I saw the dried blood.

Pulling the cloth to the center of the shed floor, I stretched its whole length out flat and walked around it, studying the pattern of the bloodstains. On the left half there was dried blood about where a man's chest would have been, a smaller amount near what would have been the position of the crossed hands, and even more spread at the feet. On the right half there was a cluster of bloodspots at the position of the head, more was matted at a point near the lower back, and again at the feet there was a heavy concentration—the bloodstain of the left foot was incomplete and slightly off-line. Some vague body stains confirmed this unmistakable pattern.

There could be no doubt. This was the same gravecloth I had held in my own hands on Friday. The realization brought an unexpected twinge of regret. I had begun to hope that somehow Peter himself was not involved, but now . . . rolling the cloth up again I told Rhoda I would take it with me. I wanted to show it to Peter. She nodded and turned back to her laundry.

I found them all still in the room where I'd left them. Magdalene was sitting hunched in Peter's chair, quieter now but still agitated. Bending over her, clasping her hands, was Peter. At the side of the chair John crouched nervously while the others hovered round. As I walked in Peter was talking, trying to soothe the woman. Abruptly, without apology, I interrupted. "Can someone else tend to her, Peter? I must have a word with you."

He answered over his shoulder, still bent. "Couldn't we do it a little later, if you don't mind?"

"No. It must be now. Immediately."

His head came round sharply and his eyes met and held mine. Then they dropped to the bulky roll under my arm. With a touch of irritation he asked as he stood up, "Yes, what is it?"

"Is there another room? I'd like some privacy."

He motioned Andrew to take his place with Magdalene, then turned to lead the way. I started to follow, then stopped and said, "John, too. Ask John to join us, please."

We followed him down the hall and entered a small, narrow room containing almost no furniture, only some chairs and a long worktable set against the far wall. As soon as Peter closed the door and turned to face me, I took the rolled cloth in both hands, held it toward him and said, "This is the linen I put round his body in the tomb. You agree?"

He reached over and fingered an edge of the roll, raising it until he saw the bloodstains. "Yes, it is. Rhoda was going to wash off the blood before we packed it away. The women thought they'd like to keep it. Oh, but it belongs to Joseph, doesn't it? Well, we'll ask him."

I could hold back no longer. "Stop it, Peter. It's all over. Your pathetic hoax is finished. You and your people took the body from the tomb. Your possession of this cloth proves it beyond question."

"Proves we took the body?" His brow furrowed. "What are you talking about? How does it prove it?"

"I'm amazed to think you kept it here so openly. But I'll waste no more time with you. That was a crime against Roman law, grave robbing, especially violating a corpse. The temple police will also be quite interested in this cloth. But we can deal with that later. What have you done with the body?"

"How does it prove it?"

"As an officer of the council, Peter, I demand to know where you have hidden the corpse."

He stood there looking at me, scarcely managing to hide his own rising anger. Then he suddenly turned away, at the same time growling in the direction of young John, "You tell him." Stalking over to the corner, he took a chair and sat down heavily, ignoring the creaking of the thin wood under his massive frame. I turned to face John, wondering what story they had concocted between them. The young man wasn't as coolheaded as his chief. He looked wary and uncertain even before he started.

"We found the cloth there this morning, sir, at the tomb. Peter and me. But what do you mean about the body? Why would we take the body?"

"Tell me about the cloth, son. Tell me exactly where you found it in the tomb, how it lay and so on."

"Lying right on the stone slab where the body was. Peter went in and I followed him and we saw it there stretched out on the stone slab." His soft tone and innocent expression blended in a wonderful show of youthful sincerity.

"How do you mean stretched out?"

"You know, stretched out . . . along the top of the slab . . . like it was ready for a corpse."

"Like it was ready. I see. You mean doubled over, half underneath, half on top, all very neat."

"Well, no sir, I'm . . ."

"Here, show me. That table there. Take the cloth. Spread it out as you remember it. Go on."

He accepted the roll, a bit hesitantly I noted, and laid it down at one end of the table. Very deliberately he unrolled it to half its length, then he stopped. For several seconds he stood there uncertainly, his eyes moving from one end to the other and back again. "It's hard to remember about the top half. Might have been pulled down, lying flat over the bottom. But maybe it was sort of thrown up, rumpled or folded or something. I don't remember about that. The small cloths, the ones from the chin and the wrists, were lying off to one side"—he pointed across the cloth about midway of its length, to the far side of the table—"not lying with the big cloth or on it. They were kind of rolled up in a place by themselves at the back of the niche."

"Go on."

"We took all of the cloths and left. I guess it seemed like something to do. I mean, you just look at that cloth, the blood and the stains, and you wonder, you know?"

Here was no novice. For all his youth, he was proving as adept with a lie as Peter. But the growing list of spurious details had begun to fascinate me, and of course like all liars the more he talked the more tangled he would become in his own web. "What do you mean, the small cloths were rolled up by themselves?"

"I mean lying apart, not right next to the shroud. Maybe a foot away. And sort of folded together."

"And you saw some significance in those small cloths lying as they were, apart like that, and rolled up?"

"Well, right now I can't say . . . I'm not sure. But yes, at the time it did seem, well, significant . . . but I don't know . . . maybe it was nothing. . . ." His voice trailed off lamely.

"Maybe nothing indeed." I faced toward Peter in the corner. "I suppose you agree with all this?"

He let loose an annoyed sigh, rose from his chair, and started for the door. "That's the way we found the cloths. Listen, Nicodemus, I've had about enough, though I don't entirely blame you. It's been an ordeal for everyone. But let's end it here."

I too was ready to put an end to the farce.

"Peter, what do you think? Say some men were robbing a tomb in the dead of night. Say the tomb was surrounded by guards, where the slightest noise or mishap could bring detection and arrest. Would the thieves take time to remove the body from the shroud, then waste more time unbinding the jaws and the wrists? Or would they simply take the body as it was, shroud and all?"

He stopped and turned around but didn't answer.

"And if we later discover this very same shroud in the hands of the dead man's friends, what then? May we not conclude that there's a close connection between the two, the friends and the missing body?"

He still didn't answer, only threw me a look of vague discomfort as he started for the door again. I went on, my voice gradually rising until I was almost shouting. "You asked if I thought you were a half-wit. No, I don't. I think you're a scoundrel! A wicked, scheming scoundrel! It's no accident about that poor, babbling woman in the other room. You've talked to her before, I see. Very patient, very insinuating. Oh, very! You'll soon have them all believing it. They taught you more things than just fishing on your lake up north. But why, Peter, why? You were the closest to him. He trusted you. And now you dishonor his memory? How can you be so misguided . . . so . . . evil!"

Brawny arms folded, Peter stood silent, staring glumly at the floor. His retreat into speechlessness didn't surprise me, but I wished fervently that I could know what was going on in his head. For some moments, the three of us stood there unmoving. Then I realized how foolish it was to hope for an instant confession. I went over to the table, took hold of one end of the cloth and quickly rolled it up. "As an officer of the council I'm confiscating this. It's evidence."

Taking one small, unhurried step toward me, Peter gave a slight shake of his head. I stopped, looked at him, then tossed the cloth back onto the table. "Very well, but be careful you don't, shall we say, lose it somehow."

I turned and walked briskly toward the door.

"Nicodemus?"

Peter's voice. I paused without looking round, my hand grasping the knob.

"The stone. What about moving the stone?"

As I closed the door behind me I could hear the testy remark of Vinucius again: there are ways.

◆

THE BEST HAND I KNOW for getting a job done quietly and efficiently, without needing every last detail explained, is my man Hazor. He manages my olive groves, and he knows everything about the business, from the growing, to the mechanics of the presses and the coring machines, to proper storage of the oil amphoras in a ship's hold. He's also up on science and history and he speaks several languages. Where he managed to learn it all I don't know, for he had few advantages to start with and he's still a year or two from thirty. There aren't many like him these days.

My only reservation, not that it matters right now, is his interest in Naomi. To be frank, Sarah and I both feel that she has much better prospects, or I should say will have, for after all she's not yet sixteen, a lovely girl but hardly ready for such things. Anyway, I understand that she's not the only young woman to have caught Hazor's eye. In fact, the way they all respond to his confident manner, those calm, brown eyes and that easy smile, he could have his pick of a dozen charming girls on his own level tomorrow.

The morning after my meeting with Peter, I sent for Hazor. When he arrived at the villa in mid-afternoon we retreated to my study and went right to work. I had two assignments in mind, I told him, and both were far from ordinary. When I described them he didn't hesitate, though perhaps he did blink a little at the second. I couldn't blame him.

The way he tackled preparations for the first assignment was a pleasure to see. Clearing off a broad table, he asked for a map of the Jerusalem environs, large scale. When it was brought he spread it on the table and began laying out on it a series of measured squares—so many hundred yards this way, so many hundred yards that way, all neatly marked down. Every foot of the Bethany road was accounted for, taking in a quarter-mile strip along either side. Then he scribbled some calculations and finally said, "We can do the job in ten days, using twenty men. There's some difference in wages between using our own men from the groves or hiring others, but for reliability I prefer our own."

Impressed, I agreed.

"We'll begin the search at Bethany instead of at this end," he went on, "since it's probable that the thieves would have wanted to get some distance away before reburying the body."

That made good sense.

"As we go along, we'll look for revealing signs in the more obscure localities, freshly turned earth, newly sealed graves, suspicious cart tracks, that sort of thing. We'll question all residents, and keep a detailed record of our findings for analysis later. We'll be ready to start in two days, at sunup." While the search was under way, he added, he'd report to me only if something interesting was found.

Rolling up the map, he asked for details of the second assignment. Before responding, I assured him that he was at perfect liberty to decline, since it involved some real hazard, at least potentially. The warning brought a glint to his alert, brown eyes.

"It means your losing a night's sleep, and I should tell you that neither Pilate nor Caiaphas will be amused if they hear of it. You'll need to do some study beforehand, and you'll also require some help. Here it is—I'd like you to devise a method for stealing a dead body from a closed and guarded tomb."

I noted only a sharpening of the gaze on the frank face.

"I don't plan to steal an actual body, just want to find how it might be done. The hard part will be moving that stone. That's the crux. The stone must be moved without causing the slightest noise, or almost none. Then I'll want you to give me a full-scale demonstration, with a tomb I'll select. We'll do it at night. Well?"

"When would you like to have the demonstration?"

"When can you be ready?"

"Give me a week, sir, if that's all right. But I should know something about the size and placement of the stone."

"You're welcome to inspect the tomb itself. All right, then, in a week from today you'll come here with your method worked out, and we'll arrange to set up the demonstration."

Folding his arms, he leaned back in his chair, his eyes traveling vacantly around the floor as his left thumb rubbed along his jaw. Then he dropped his hand and bent forward. "What about this, sir? When I'm ready I will not come here, but will send you a note. That night late, you and several others go to Golgotha, say a little before midnight. Set yourselves up some distance off, where you can't see the tomb. Then wait. If you hear a sound from the tomb during the night, it will mean I've failed, and you may come up immediately. If you hear nothing, come to the tomb after sunrise."

This was perfect. "Good! And I'll disperse my people just as the guards were . . . no, wait. It's better if you're ignorant of all that. And to make it realistic we'll use a large sandbag to simulate the body. How would that be? Before we settle down we'll place the sandbag in the tomb and close the stone. Good!"

Asking him to wait, I went down the hall to the office to get the money he'd need. I was gone about ten minutes. When I returned, there was Naomi, serving him wine and talking in quite a relaxed and friendly fashion. She happened to be passing, she said, saw Hazor alone, and decided to keep our guest company till I got back. I said that was very gracious of her, and I could see that Hazor thought so too. I also noticed she was wearing one of her best dresses, which she had not been wearing an hour before.

◆

T*HAT ROGUE PETER* didn't waste any time. As I heard later, his shocking campaign of deception began not long after I left him. It seems that my unexpected presence at his house that day even delayed his plans. I was only an inconvenience, not a threat. No wonder he seemed so patient, no wonder he got rid of me as soon as he could. And I thought he was tongue-tied with guilt! It's amazing to think that Caiaphas was right after all.

What takes my breath away is the ingenious scope of it all, the sheer execution. It's plain to see how Peter arranged everything for maximum effect, building his little drama in three stages, all packed into a single day, all mounting to a crescendo of excitement. Something of the basic pattern I can trace, but I still can't decide how he was able to bring off the stunning finale. This is a far more resourceful man than he seems, with that gentle-giant manner.

I record the three-event pattern as it was pieced together for me some days afterward on information supplied by a number of the Galileans who were present. They were only too happy to babble about what happened, and of course they had no idea they were talking to two of my agents.

The curtain raiser, which took place in the upper room less than two hours after my departure, featured Peter himself in a solitary role. He carried the part off to perfection, it seems, revealing unsuspected talents.

Silence had descended on the house and for a while nothing stirred. Then Peter in great agitation came hurrying to the upper room, where he called his scattered group together. Standing before them with eyes aglow, in a trembling voice he gave out the astounding news that, like Magdalene, he had seen the risen Jesus, seen him not as a ghost but in the flesh. It had happened only minutes before, he solemnly declared, while he was praying alone in one of the private rooms—serene and smiling and friendly, Jesus had stood right there in front of him offering sympathy and encouragement.

Of course, Peter's dramatic announcement had a profound effect on all present. Instantly the atmosphere in the house was charged with a tense combination of wonder, suspense, and expectation. (One thing I do find curious: though my men asked, no conversation was reported for Peter's meeting with his reanimated chief. Why didn't the resourceful Peter invent a full script, complete with dialogue? Using just a little imagination . . . well, he's human after all, and for this day's work he had quite a bit on his mind!)

The second act began later that same evening, and it was a

rouser, worthy to be ranked with the best Roman drama. I say this sincerely.

After supper the group—some thirty men, I understand—took its ease lolling behind the locked doors of the upper room, talking in wonderment about Peter's experience earlier. Suddenly, the silence was shattered as there came a furious pounding on the door. Hastily it was unlocked and thrown open, upon which two men, disheveled and agitated, tumbled in. They proved to be two of their own number who had left Jerusalem that morning for their homes in a nearby village. Quickly the doors were shut and locked again, and the two excited travelers proceeded to tell their little tale. I give the gist of it.

"We were walking along the road toward Emmaus," one said, "when we were overtaken by a friendly stranger, a man who ventured to inquire what we were looking so glum about." The two described for the stranger the horror of Jesus' crucifixion, and they also told how greatly disappointed and crushed they were, since it had seemed to everyone that Jesus was the Messiah. "Then the stranger chimed in. From memory he quoted scripture after scripture on the Messiah, a long list of passages with what seemed remarkable links to Jesus"—a feat that soon had the two listening openmouthed.

At Emmaus, reluctant to part from their intriguing new acquaintance, they invited him to stay to supper. But at table, instead of acting like a guest, the stranger indulged in behavior that took everyone by surprise. "He picked up the bread himself, blessed it, broke it, then handed the pieces around to all in turn!" As he did so, in a flash the two men at last recognized the true identity of their remarkable companion—guess who! But in that very instant Jesus vanished from the room: "One moment he was sitting there, the next he was gone" (why he should have decamped so fast is not explained). As soon as they recovered their wits the two jumped up and rushed pell-mell back to Jerusalem.

That charming tale, coming on top of Peter's own opening tableau, cleverly set the stage for the grand climax. After hearing two such thrilling reports, who could hope to think rationally when caught up in the sensation that next unfolded in that upper room?

While the two from Emmaus were breathlessly answering the questions being thrown at them from every side, someone in the crush shouted loudly, in his voice a shrill note of alarm. The hubbub ceased abruptly, all eyes on the shouter. Then in the stillness all heads swung round—and there, standing in solitary state at the far end of the locked room, was none other than Jesus. Rather than rushing forward to greet their returned leader—which you'd expect after what they'd just heard—the whole milling bunch sank back as one toward the barred doors, mumbling and muttering in fright about spirits (Peter's job with this motley crew wasn't easy!).

The apparition spoke. "Come see my hands and feet," it said, "touch me and see. A spirit doesn't have flesh and bones as you can see that I have."

At first none dared accept this, to say the least, unique invitation. Eventually one or two of them inched forward hesitantly, then a few others followed, and gradually all began to calm down. Nobody had nerve enough to touch the apparition, however, or even to approach it, nor could they bring themselves to believe what they saw, or thought they saw. As one of them said afterward, they were simply afraid to trust their own senses in anything so strange, so stupendous, especially something so near their own hearts. They all "disbelieved for joy," was how he put it. Personally I found that phrase quite a nice touch.

The apparition next asked for some food, presumably as a way of convincing his doubtful audience he was real. Handed a plate of fish (not actually handed: the cook just put a plate down at one end of a long table and gave it a little shove), he ate it standing there in plain sight. Chewing slowly as if savoring each bite, he looked deliberately around at the men, at one point asking if there was any salt. Then he set the empty plate down on the table, and poured and drank a small glass of wine.

That loosened things up and the rest of the evening was spent with Jesus teaching and interpreting scripture. At one point he announced they were all to become witnesses of what he called his resurrection, and he backed this up by imparting to every last man in the room the wholesale power to forgive sins! All present, it appears, took very much in stride this sudden leap from lowly fishmonger all the way up to judge of Israel. And beyond, apparently.

The first two stages of this little drama hardly need comment. Given collusion, enough planning and preparation, and Peter's skillful direction, they would have been pretty easily managed (it wouldn't hurt, now that I think of it, to send a man out to check on the Emmaus incident, get an affidavit from that householder if he can be found). The third is more troublesome.

Assume that it's not just a case of concerted lying—a very difficult theory in itself since it would be far from simple to work up a conspiracy of this delicate kind with thirty tongues to be coached and manipulated and watched. Assume that every man who was in the room that evening believed that he saw Jesus in the flesh, watched him eat, heard him talk. Was it wholesale self-delusion, possibly? A mad product of the yearning imagination, simple-hearted people seeing what they wanted to see? The Greeks describe a mental condition they call hysteria, which may well fit this case. But how was it created? How was it sustained for so long, two hours or more? Are these so-called hysterics able to disbelieve for joy? I would think that to doubt the evidence of your own eyes you need self-possession, a level head.

The most reasonable answer is the use of an imposter. Someone, a clever mimic, of about the same appearance as Jesus, well coached for the role, could have been let into the room by a confederate while attention was diverted over the Emmaus excitement. The staging would have been easy—a few small lamps and candles giving a murky light, a hood shading the imposter's face, no one allowed to get too near him, and so on. Yet there's a problem.

These men have had almost daily contact with Jesus for—what was it, three years? If a muffled figure made some kind of a sensational entrance, then quickly exited amid the uproar, maybe they could have been fooled for a while. But a calm two hours with the imposter standing and talking there in full view? Say it was only an hour. Say it was a half hour or even ten minutes. Could any man no matter how clever have impersonated this Jesus under sustained scrutiny?

A conspiracy, mass hallucination, an imposter. Which? At the moment I'm still unable to choose and can think of no others. In the end, I wonder if it really matters.

◆

HAZOR, *AS I SHOULD HAVE EXPECTED,* wasted no time. His note arrived early on the morning of the sabbath and was brought to me promptly. It was brief: "I am ready. Tonight."

This meant that our experiment at the tomb would take place on the same day as that on which the body had been stolen, but one week later. Such precision of detail at least gave the affair a certain feeling of tidiness, assuring that we hadn't overlooked anything.

The team of men who'd play the Roman guards I had already recruited, from my staff at the villa. The exact conditions of that night couldn't be reproduced, of course, but to get close I chose the more lethargic men, those not accustomed to missing a night in bed. Over his groaning protests my excellent gardener, Levi, was included. This is a man who could slumber comfortably through an earthquake, so I asked him to take the place of one of the two guards who'd been on duty at the tomb. He gave his consent but his manner of doing so could not be termed gracious! The other of the two guards at the tomb would be Jotham, one of the younger stable hands who is not known for vigor, which puts it mildly, and who readily agreed on hearing he would have the next day free. These two were the nearest I could get to what Vinucius reported as the exhausted condition of the two Roman guards standing that watch.

The sandbag that would substitute for the body had also been prepared, a special one of heavy cloth made up for me by Sarah and the girls. Nearly six feet long and about two feet wide, when filled it weighed close to two hundred pounds, which seemed about right. The sand to fill it the men would carry to Golgotha in smaller bags, much neater, no shovels, no digging, no noise.

When Hazor's note came I sent word to all six men to assemble here in my study at nine that evening, bringing with them their sacks of sand. My plan was to leave for Golgotha soon after nine, for I was determined to be settled in place well before midnight. I wanted to avoid any rush, either on the trip out or in the business of selecting a position near the tomb.

Feeling more anxious by the minute, I prepared to spend an interminable day of waiting, nervous waiting I knew it would be, since my mind quickly grew fidgety and refused to concern itself with ordinary affairs of any kind. And there were some twelve hours to go! Never has an hour in prospect seemed so long to me, and I confess that I fairly rattled around the house from study to kitchen, getting in everybody's way and upsetting the servants with my sudden appearances. Rather dramatically, all of that changed in early afternoon when I received an unexpected visitor. For a while I actually forgot all about what was to happen that night at Golgotha.

It was one of Peter's men, the one they call the Twin, known as Thomas. I had seen him several times but had never spoken with him directly. He's a quiet, brooding type, with a sharp face and sallow skin, the kind that sees everything, says little, scarcely allows himself a spontaneous moment. When he arrived and was announced, curbing my surprise I bade him welcome, sat him down in the study, and called for some fruit and wine. I was at his service, I assured him.

Abruptly, without preliminaries, he announced what he had come for: to tell me that I was completely and egregiously wrong about the Galileans' having stolen the body. "Possession of the cloth proves nothing!" he burst out. "Nothing at all!" His friends couldn't have done such a ghoulish thing, he insisted, they weren't benighted savages. "Furthermore," he went rushing on before I could open my mouth, "I'm here to speak for my friends even though I do *not* believe that Jesus appeared to them in that upper room."

At this outright confession I admit that I gaped a bit. Then came a tremendous flood of relief: here at last was the first real break in the case—one of their own number had come forward to repudiate the terrible hoax. Perhaps others would follow Thomas's lead, and the whole cabal would collapse. Curbing my rising excitement, I suppressed the many questions that leaped to mind and waited patiently for my guest to go on.

Speaking precisely, his thin voice again under control, he explained that he had not been present in the upper room that evening. "I couldn't just sit there dumbly with the others, so I went out and made an effort to trace the missing body on my own. I questioned everybody I could think of, including the Golgotha caretakers and the watchmen at the three western gates. When I got back to the house late that night everyone descended on me shouting that Jesus was alive and had talked to them in that very room."

At first he was thunderstruck, he said, unable to speak. Then recovering, he demanded angrily of his friends why no one had done the intelligent thing. "If the apparition really did invite them to come forward and examine him," he said in a pained tone while looking at me rather helplessly, "why wasn't it done? They are asked to believe the most extraordinary fact ever heard since the world began, and what do they do? Nothing but cower and stare!" He dropped his eyes to his hands where they rested on his knees and muttered "Incredible!"

In spite of his friends' efforts to convince him, in spite of Peter's own quiet assurances, he had stubbornly held out. He would not and he could not believe such a thing, he insisted, without clear and convincing evidence, the sort that left no shadow of doubt. For him, that meant nothing less than a close inspection of the raw wounds. His final answer to his friends, as he repeated it to me, was emphatic: "Unless I see in his hands the print of the nails, and place my finger in the mark of the nails, and place my hand in his side, I will not believe." Stressing the "will not," as he pronounced each word he angrily chopped his open hand edgewise through the air.

Here was a staunch man of reason, I thought as I listened to him, a man of true intellect, sound in character. Quite rightly, he knew that the eyes can deceive the mind, that there's less chance for deception when eyes and hands work together. This Thomas proves a rare find indeed. What strength of will it must have taken to resist the flood of cajolery from his deluded friends!

I was not in a mood right then to press my own opinions. That would have spoiled the moment for me, certainly would have antagonized him. Refusing all food and drink, he departed, satisfied that I would keep an open mind, and feeling that he had at least come to his friends' defense in a matter that could well threaten their personal safety.

◆

GOLGOTHA AT NIGHT is a lonely place. Even in the dark the high city wall can be felt, or sensed, looming over it black and ponderous. Anyone whose business takes him there so late can hardly miss the chill feeling of being shut away from all human sympathy. Soft noises dimly afloat on the air, the last faint stirrings in the city's deserted streets, drift over the wall and sift down through the shadows.

It was after ten when the seven of us converged on the tomb. We had left the villa separately by twos, myself alone, following different routes. We had even exited the city by three different gates. That way the watchmen saw nothing to disturb their night's vigil.

At the tomb we gathered quietly in the small vestibule. Working in silence by the feeble light of a small, shielded torch, the men filled the large sack with sand, stopping when it was reasonably plump and firm throughout, yet not rigid. At either end they tied ropes around it to give a grip. Dragging it through the low doorway into the burial chamber, they hoisted it, not without a few involuntary grunts, up onto the same stone slab where his body had lain. Of course, the sack had no appendages to take the place of arms and legs, and to that extent the experiment might be deemed faulty. But we agreed that this wasn't crucial.

Moving out from the chamber to the vestibule, the men carefully rolled down the big stone. I stood back and listened as they hauled on it, taking a mental note of the familiar loud rumbling and scraping sound it made as they wrestled it into position. When it came to rest we made sure it sat tight against the wall.

Next I directed the placement of the pseudo-guards. With the good Levi, I climbed the hill behind the tomb and found a comfortable depression lined with grass about halfway up. There I invited him to bed down, a task he accomplished only after a truly elaborate series of bodily maneuvers accompanied by groans and sighs, all meant to impress me with the extraordinary sacrifice he was making—and which, if I know my old Levi, he will certainly bring to my attention whenever he needs some leverage. Vertically, measuring straight up from the ground, his position lay about fifteen feet higher than the tomb's roof. The actual distance down the slanting hill to the door of the tomb of course was longer, about forty feet.

Standing to the tomb's right on level ground was the large bush that Vinucius had mentioned. It was the only one of any size along the hill's base, less than thirty feet away from the vestibule. There I placed the sluggish Jotham, who expressed his pleasure at finding under him a level mattress of thick grass. Contentedly he snuggled down wrapped in his heavy blanket.

With the four other men, I walked west from the tomb to where the small brook ran through the thin clump of trees. From that spot only the left side of the vestibule could be glimpsed, and then only if there was some light. Under cover of darkness, the vestibule and the entire tomb structure blended into the black bulk of the hill rising over and around it.

In a few minutes the men had rigged a simple sleeping tent for me, made from a large blanket hung on a rope strung between some tree branches stuck into the ground. I had debated bringing along my own spacious tent that I've had for years, with a comfortable cot, which would match the centurion's arrangement. Then I decided that the blanket and the ground would do as well, since I was not expecting to sleep much anyway.

Nearby we found the remains of the Romans' cooking fire from that night, so our spot had been well chosen. When we had a small flame going, I positioned the four men around the fire to sleep. Gratefully they dropped to the ground, wrapped themselves in their double cloaks, and pulled woolen hoods over their heads. The empty sandbags they folded up for pillows. Unlike real guards, I reminded them, on this job they were encouraged to sleep—I wanted them all to be sound asleep between midnight and dawn. But it was very important that if some noise did awaken them, anything at all, they were to get up immediately and report to me. "Yes, sir. Thank you, sir," they mumbled in chorus, their minds already drifting off.

For a while, snugly wrapped in robes and hood, I sat relaxing on the ground in front of my makeshift tent, enjoying the coolish solitude. Some few night birds were in the area, and their delicate chirping joined the occasional sharper double note of the cricket to create a subtle harmony. It made a soothing music, if a little melancholy—just the sort of serene and pensive atmosphere that when younger I used to yearn for, and which has sadly eluded me of late years. Heart-stilling moods, I called them. I suppose that's the price we pay for being creatures of intellect, for bowing to the claims of duty and responsibility. Pressed and harried by the steady advance of life, simplicity gives way to increasing involvement and complication, no doubt as it must. The heart itself constricts, and even the eyes see not what once they saw. Was it ever any different? Here in the dark, sheltered beneath the shadowy rise of Golgotha, for a while anyway it seemed different. Really quite peaceful.

What woke me, I can't tell. Suddenly I found myself lying there, my eyes wide open, wondering why I couldn't see the familiar white-patterned ceiling of my bedroom. What was this pall of darkness so ominously near my face? With a start I realized I was stretched full length on the hard ground, half underneath my little tent. Then I remembered—the tomb! Hurriedly I struggled to push myself from under the draped blanket, feeling the soreness in my hips as I rolled over.

It was morning. The sun, blurred and hazy, had begun its climb. As I rose to my feet I turned and looked toward the fire. The four men were still sprawled around it, still lost in sleep. I swung around and looked toward the tomb, but could see only the side of the vestibule. "You men," I shouted to the four, "wake up! Wake up!" Not waiting for a response, I gathered up the edge of my robe and ran for the tomb.

Rounding the vestibule corner I almost fell down as I skidded to a stop in front of the entrance, my eyes searching the shadows inside. Sleep, and the sun's misty glare, made my vision swim for a moment, and I squinted and strained, able to see nothing clearly. Rubbing my eyes vigorously, I peered hard.

The stone was still in place. Hadn't been moved an inch, hadn't been touched, so far as I could tell. It stood there just as we had placed it the night before.

Backing off a few feet I looked up the hill behind the tomb. Tottering on the grassy slope was Levi, making his slow and painful way down over the rough surface. I threw a glance to the right, toward the bush where Jotham had slept. He was just sitting up and stretching his long arms, his mouth gaping in a yawn. Behind me the other four men came noisily crowding up.

What had happened? If no sound from the tomb had disturbed us, then Hazor should have succeeded. The big stone should be standing to one side, leaving the chamber entrance wide open. Obviously, none of us had been awakened. But where was Hazor? Had he tried the tomb and given up in defeat?

"Over here, sir!"

The shout came from the trees off to the right. We all swung round and there, smiling brightly as he walked toward us, was Hazor. "Have a good sleep?" he asked.

"Well, Hazor," I said as he came up, "I'll admit I'm puzzled. You not only failed, it looks as if you never really tried. We'd have heard you, wouldn't we? What went wrong?"

"Sir, I invite your attention to the man coming around the hill behind me."

I glanced over Hazor's shoulder to the far side of the hill. A man trundling a rickety wheelbarrow came slowly into view. As he approached nearer we were able to see the contents of the barrow. It was a large sandbag.

"You opened the tomb and then closed it again?"

"Yes, sir, and the whole operation, including removal of the sandbag, took just under two minutes. We finished three hours ago. I was wondering if you'd ever wake up."

"As easy as all that?"

"Easy to execute, yes, but the planning was everything. What threw me off at first was your way of stating the problem. Silent removal of the *stone*, you said. But that wasn't it. The problem was silent removal of the *body*. All we had to do was gain an opening large enough to admit a man. You'd be surprised how little space that requires."

"Yes, of course. Very perceptive. But how . . ."

"First I took a small chunk of the stone and weighed it, and from that I calculated the weight of the whole stone, a rough figure but pretty close. Came out at something over sixteen hundred pounds. This meant that if we pulled the *top* of the stone back from the wall a distance of about three feet—leaving the *bottom* in place but pulling the *top* back—the weight to be sustained would be only four hundred pounds." He emphasized the "four," making it contrast with the "sixteen," then he paused and looked at me expectantly.

"How did you get that?" I obliged.

"Figured it from the angle of lean, a little over thirty degrees. Two husky men could easily take four hundred pounds on their backs while we jammed two thick poles in place for props. Needed two to keep the stone from wobbling as we climbed in over it at the side."

"Hazor," I said, shaking my head, "you really should have been here when they were building the temple."

"Wish I had been! Of course, the aperture between the wall and the slanting stone was widest at the top. The entrance to the chamber was lower down, where the aperture narrowed, but we still had enough room for a man to slip in. Two of us entered. We hauled the sandbag out and had it on its way in the wheelbarrow in about a minute. Oh, yes—under the stone's bottom edge, where it pivoted in the groove as the top came back, we inserted a thick piece of well-oiled leather. Did away with any scraping. Wasn't even a squeak."

The feat was remarkable and I said so. Yet even as Hazor talked I began to see that it didn't quite fit the case. The women had found the tomb wide open, not closed. The stone itself they had found leaning against the wall to the left of the entrance. I mentioned the point to Hazor.

"I was aware of that, sir, but in our talk you didn't specify. So I decided to show how the grave robbers might have done a really impressive piece of work, if they had taken the time to use some imagination—a man rising from the dead and leaving his sealed-up tomb without bothering to open it—right through solid stone. You see? Very mysterious. These Galileans must all be plodders."

"Far from plodders, Hazor. Later I'll tell you about the latest little fantasy they've cooked up. Or have you heard?"

"Uh, well, yes, I did. That is, I mean I've heard something." The hesitating manner was unlike him.

"I thought you might. How *do* you get hold of these things so fast anyway? Does everyone in Jerusalem confide in you?"

"No, sir," he said, suppressing a grin. "But I have many men under me, and they all have families, and families have friends, who also have families." He stopped and flicked an appraising glance at me. "But, uh, this time . . . this time it wasn't any of them. No. You see, Naomi and I . . ."

"Naomi?"

"Yes. She told me."

"Did she? I don't remember you being over at the villa lately."

"It was at the grove, sir, the new grove. She came out there one day. For a visit. She and Rebecca."

"I see. Does she go out there often?"

"Oh, no . . . not what you'd call *often.* But she likes to hear about how everything works, the growing and . . . the pressing . . . and so on."

"Doesn't get in your way, I hope."

"Never, sir. A sensible girl."

"Yes, very sensible, For her age. A pretty thing, too, isn't she?"

"Well, you know, you could even say she's, well, almost beautiful, couldn't you? Not like a child, I mean . . ."

"Now, listen, Hazor, what about moving that stone off to the side, instead of pulling it back? Think you could do it that way too if you had to?"

He quickly turned away, not quite able to hide a look of relief. Raising an arm high over his head, he motioned in the direction of the trees. Another man stepped into view and came forward. He was carrying a small, flat, cloth-wrapped bundle. "You and the men can stay here if you like, sir," Hazor said, "but I'll ask you all to turn your backs."

Motioning to his two helpers, he entered the vestibule. The rest of us turned away and faced out toward the clump of trees. As the seconds passed, aside from a slight shuffling of feet, I heard only a single low grunt. Then there was a very light scraping noise, like a whisper of wind, that would have been inaudible twenty feet away. There came the sound of more footsteps and then Hazor was standing beside me.

"Sorry for the scraping. Sand."

I turned. The stone was sitting to one side, the left, entirely exposing the chamber entrance. I walked into the vestibule and saw that the groove beneath the stone was lined with leather.

"These did the trick," Hazor said, holding out both hands. In one lay two small, leather-covered spheres. The other held a narrow length of metal, also encased in leather, five inches wide and about a foot long, with a low, inverted V-shaped hump near one end. "We'll show you."

He directed his men to set the stone back in place. Three of them took hold and wrestled it down the slight incline, creating that familiar rumbling, grating noise as it inched along the rough wall and groove. Once it was set, Hazor stepped up with the length of metal and laid it down carefully, pushing an edge beneath the stone's curving left side. Then two of the men, using stout sticks, pried the stone's top slightly away from the wall. Deftly, Hazor wedged the two spheres in between wall and stone, about a foot apart, and the sticks were removed. "Now," Hazor instructed, and the two men bent to the stone's right side.

Gently they heaved against the ponderous weight as Hazor pressed in on the stone's top, keeping it in contact with the spheres. Slowly the stone shifted, rode up and over the slight hump in the metal piece, then rolled easily and silently off to the side.

Part II

THERE HAS BEEN A CHANGE, a drastic change, one I would never have foreseen at the start. Like it or not, I'm now forced to concede at least the possibility that the body—ah! but this will never do! My thoughts are in a jumble, rushing ahead of one another. If this record is to make any sense at all I must slow down. Everything that has happened in the past three weeks, since our experiment with the stone, must be given calmly and in order.

It was only a day or two after that night at the tomb that we were startled to discover Peter's absence from Jerusalem. With his whole band he had cleared out, vanished, completely and without warning. At the big house only the regulars were left—Mark, his mother, and Rhoda. It was only by accident that I found this out, as a result of looking over some notes I had made earlier. When I heard about it I felt like a fool, I could so easily have set a man to watch them.

Browsing through the notes, I found myself lingering over Joanna's remark about the young man at the tomb, the one wearing the bright garb. For the first time I began to wonder just who this stranger could have been. How had he been able to wander about the area so freely? Where had he gone afterward? What was all this about his moonglow attire? As the picture of that busy morning at the tomb assembled itself in my mind, its real complications finally dawned: from the various statements made to me, it was clear that all these comings and goings had actually taken place at almost the same time, the same moment. Yet, curiously, none of these people had met or seen each other.

In Joanna's own words, she and the other women had arrived at Golgotha "early, just before sunup." But Vinucius said the same thing—the two sleeping guards and the empty tomb were discovered "at the change of watch, just before first light." Then the six guards began combing the area, which puts them still on the scene just at, and even after, sunrise.

Next came Magdalene, whose first visit had to be fitted in after the departure of the guards, but before the arrival of the other women—in fact, a good ten minutes before them, according to Joanna's estimate. Yet the women claimed that they had arrived at the tomb while it was still dark. To put it mildly, the pieces didn't fit, not to mention that there was precious little room left in the timetable for the intrusion of the white-robed stranger. Here we had a total of no less than fourteen people, all converging openly on one small plot of ground, seemingly at the identical moment in early morning, or just about. And there had been no encounters.

It might have happened like that, one group moving off the scene seconds or minutes before the arrival of the others. Yet the more I pondered all this traffic round the empty tomb, the more the picture disturbed me. Someone could be lying, but who? A lie seemed out of character for the fearless centurion. What would be his motive? And the same could be said for the others, what reason would they have for lying, and so clumsily? It was obvious that I needed to know much more, and to know it more exactly, in particular the details of the part played that night by the women. Or should I say that morning? Also, I had if possible to establish the identity of the young man.

To invite all six of the women to my villa for questioning, I dispatched a messenger to the big house. He was gone less than an hour, and he came back with the disturbing news that the women were nowhere to be found. Not only that, all the men were missing too. The messenger had questioned young Mark and his mother, and Rhoda, but all three had professed ignorance—the whole band had simply gone off early one morning, they said, explaining nothing, not even when they'd be back. Well, that certainly was an outright lie, but I knew better than to press the point.

My first thought was that Peter, having accomplished his purpose, had taken his men away into hiding. In his place I'd have done the same. I suppose anyone would, especially after those threats I'd made about the police and that telltale cloth. I now could have kicked myself for that bumbling exhibition I put on with Peter and John. It was an outright blunder to have revealed my evidence so soon, and it made me appreciate more than ever how really difficult is the task of the analytical detector. For one thing, the facts are not that easy to gather! And when they're all lined up you've got to know what to *do* with them. With that cloth, I should have held off until I'd had a chance to weave a stronger net for the fisherman. I won't make that mistake a second time.

The question was where? Assuming that Peter and his band had gone for good—personally I had no doubt—in what direction would those guilty men have fled? Galilee, quite likely. That seemed clear enough, a dash northward for the safety of those familiar hills crowding the lake, where they could settle in among old friends who were not inclined to talk to outsiders. From up there in Galilee, seventy or eighty miles away, Jerusalem with its prying officials would feel comfortably remote.

It wasn't until later, when Hazor came in with his final report on the Bethany search party, that I grasped the further implication of those men absconding like that. Might they not have taken the body with them? Dug it up from wherever it was hidden, bundled it into a wagon and slipped off? The more I thought about it, the more that conclusion seemed irresistible, even to the point where I was ready to act on it.

Hazor's search party did an amazingly thorough job. Still, regrettably, his time was pretty much wasted. He did turn up three fresh graves of a suspicious nature, even opened one of them. When the owners found out, of course, there was an ugly scene, leaving some bad feeling that I had to smooth over with the council. The pile of notes he took of his interviews along the way also looked promising, with their hints of furtive nighttime activity. All had quickly proved to be nothing more than the empty gossip of jealous neighbors, which surprised me more than it should have.

The day of Hazor's search party report also brought the first news from my man in Emmaus. I had sent him there on the outside chance that Peter might not have been so careful in setting things up at that end, nearly ten miles out of town, thinking that nobody would bother to check. More wasted effort. It turns out that one of the two travelers was a man named Cleopas, an uncle of Jesus, and the house in Emmaus was his. At the table that day were two other people and both swear to the story of the disappearance, but they were relatives, so we can discount them. Peter even went so far as to ring in an obliging neighbor as a witness: the man next door and his wife swear they met Cleopas coming home that Sunday and with him were two other men, one of them being a tall, coppery-haired stranger. My man thinks the neighbor wasn't lying, but was simply telling what he actually saw. That brings us back to an imposter, someone playing a part, this time an easy one, requiring nothing but a stroll in full view down a village street. As I said, it was a waste of time, but of course the effort had to be made.

◆

IN GALILEE our accommodations were definitely on the rough side: two rooms on the ramshackle top floor of a small, nondescript inn just outside Bethsaida. I'm not the fastidious type but I did heave a sigh at these dismal surroundings. The rooms were narrow, with low ceilings and inconvenient beams. The drab board walls held no plaster, the air was damp, and the loose shutters on the one tiny window in my room were forever rattling in the light wind. The bed was hard as a rock and the food atrocious—the cook's fault, since the quality wasn't bad, especially the fish, which was caught fresh daily almost at the door.

The sole redeeming feature of the place was the view, really splendid, which could have been the only reason for the high prices. The inn sat on the shore of the lake, and from my window I could look south for miles and miles over the restless, blue-black surface to where it faded far in the distance. To the right I could also make out the low profile of the coastal town of Capernaum, its white-walled houses glowing in the sun some three miles away along the curving shoreline.

We might have stayed at any of several much nicer places in Bethsaida, but that wouldn't have served our purpose. Hazor and I were now well aware that Peter and his companions had indeed headed this way, making a hasty scramble for their homes. That information was picked up—need I say it?—by Hazor through his network. One of the Galilean women doing the marketing had said good-bye to a friend and had mentioned their plans, in confidence of course. The friend promptly told her husband, the husband told his cousin, and the cousin told his brother, who happened to be a packer at my north grove. Didn't take Hazor long to root him out.

Except for Peter, we knew very little about exactly where all these men lived. Our main target was Peter, however, and we knew that he was a native of Capernaum. Somewhere in the town he had a house, we'd been told, occupied by a wife and a mother-in-law. Some said a young daughter as well.

Our initial plan was a simple one. We had arrived at the inn under cover of darkness, the better to keep secret our presence in the area. Since I might be recognized, I was to remain in my room. Hazor, who was unknown to the Galileans, would act as my eyes and ears. Posing as a fisherman seeking work, he'd go into Capernaum and poke around to see what information he could pick up, and would also locate Peter's house. When he found it, he was to observe the situation carefully for a day or so, then report back to me.

Eager as usual, early next morning Hazor was ready to go out on his mission. Attired in rough work clothes he came to my room to say he was leaving—and that's when he came up with his clever idea about the body.

As he stood gazing out the little window, he remarked offhandedly about the large number of fishing boats to be seen on the lake. "I'm surprised. So many out there in the daytime. Night fishing is the usual thing up here. Guess the water temperature has something to do with it." He turned away from the window, stopped, then quickly turned back, leaning his head out. "I think I've found the perfect place to hide a corpse," he said quietly as he drew his head in again.

I jumped up from where I'd been sitting on the bed, went to the window, put my head out and looked down. Between the inn and the shoreline there lay a margin of land some twenty yards wide, covered with a sprinkling of trees, grass and boulders. Nothing very promising there.

"Not down. Look straight out."

I lifted my eyes. Yes! The lake itself! A body well wrapped and weighted with rocks could be sunk to a great depth in those waters. Here indeed was a grave that would leave no trace.

I looked south to where the broad, shining surface disappeared on the misty horizon. The word *lake* was misleading. This was an inland sea, and in fact as often as not that's what people called it. The Sea of Galilee. Because it's so enormous, even in daylight a corpse could be smuggled out on a fishing boat to the center, then slipped overboard. No fear of anyone spotting either the deed or its perpetrators. And Peter and his bunch were fishermen, familiar with these very waters from childhood.

"But have they had a chance to do it yet?" asked Hazor, guessing my thoughts. "They've already been here for three days. If they have, then the body's gone for good. There's no case. Without a body, these men can say whatever they please. You can't arrest people for claiming they talked to a dead man." He picked up a small sack in which he had some extra clothes and slung it on his shoulder. "I'm off, sir. I should be in Capernaum before noon. I'll stay there until tomorrow night, at least. Unless something comes up, I'll see you back here then."

Not quite true, I thought as the door closed behind him, not quite true. This wasn't murder. For murder you need a body, to prove there's been a death and maybe show how it happened. This was theft, of a gruesome kind, but still theft. If a man steals a box of jewels, and then gets rid of the jewels, but you know he was in the house and later you catch him with the empty box, I'd think you have a pretty good case. Even if Peter has managed to get rid of the jewels, he has already been caught with the box. That cloth.

Earlier I had ordered breakfast brought to my room, and it came up shortly after Hazor left. When I answered a knock at the door, the proprietor's wife stood there carrying a large tray piled with dried fish, figs, olives, grapes, bread, cheese, and a small jug of wine. I let her in, glad to see the food, for I was famished, having skipped supper. As she bent down to set the tray on the narrow table by the bed she glanced shyly up from under her disheveled hair, her eyes inquisitive. I recognized the signs and I groaned to myself. I was in for some prattle, and I was in no mood for it.

"It'll be a nice day, sir," she said in a cheerful tone as she straightened up, hands smoothing her hair, "if you mean to go walking by the lake. My Jacob said it would storm, but it's turned out lovely. Thinks he can tell the weather by the color of the sunset on the water, and maybe he can, but he's been wrong all this month. You must be here on business, I suppose. These days not many come up from Jerusalem on holiday."

She waited, wiping her hands repeatedly on her apron. When I volunteered no reply, she finally started slowly for the door, mumbling just loud enough for me to hear. "Service in silence, as we say. Still, you being from Jerusalem and all . . ." Pausing, she brushed some dust from a bureau top with the apron's edge.

"Yes?" I said grudgingly. Better to answer and get rid of her once and for all.

Eagerly she turned and moved toward me, hands fluttering. "Oh, sir, were you there when they crucified him, the teacher from Nazareth, that Jesus? The talk that's going round! He's dead, he isn't dead, the body's lost, what aren't they saying! Some folks from here went down for Passover, and now that's all they talk about. Never heard of such a thing! But did you see it? I still don't understand why they had to kill him."

"You knew the man?" I was becoming curious to learn how these country people regarded him. Also, I needed time to decide on an answer that would not prolong the agony.

"Oh, no. Not likely. I did see him, two or three times. You know, they say he cured an old blind man right here in town. Oh, but you hear a lot of things like that about him." Pointing a finger toward the window, she went on. "In that little village up in the hills on the other side, they say he brought a dead man back to life. Really. Out in the street in front of everyone. They were taking the body away. A widow's son. Well, I mean!"

This was a story I hadn't heard. It brought to mind the wild rumor that had sped around Jerusalem shortly before he was executed, about that friend in Bethany. There was also that other incident of the same kind, a little girl, and I've heard talk of still others. Wonderful how these tales are apt to grow up around a striking personality, exaggerations of some simple incident. I've often thought that someone ought to collect these stories and study them, trace them back to their sources. Might learn something about how the minds of the ignorant work. I don't mean the ordinary healings that so many have reported. They're different of course.

"Anyway, he said nice things," the woman continued. "One day we all went over to the big hill to see him, a whole crowd. When he talked, sitting up there on the hill and looking down at us, he made you feel good. Not so tired, you know?"

"What else have you heard about him?"

"Oh, you can't believe everything. My Jacob says it's mostly just talk. He says if they had let the man alone, not go running after him, it would've been all right. Once it got started, my Jacob says, him healing people and everyone chasing after him and all, well, it was bound to get out of hand. The priests didn't like it, my Jacob says, and they had lots of arguments, him and the priests. But did they really kill him?"

"I'm afraid it's true that he's dead. He died on a cross along with two others. I happened to be there myself. He was buried, all right. As your Jacob says, the rest is just talk, madam, just talk."

I sat down by the tray, picked up a piece of fish and started eating. My good landlady took the hint at last, but reluctantly, for at the door she paused and looked around, as if ready with another question. Then she changed her mind and walked out.

◆

A *HAND GRASPING* my shoulder woke me. In the darkness of the room the intense glare of a candle held near my face caused me to blink rapidly. As I struggled to raise myself on the pillow, I saw Hazor's eyes gleaming beside the small flame. "Quiet, sir," he whispered, "be quiet, but hurry and get your clothes on. I'll explain later."

My nerves humming, I was up and dressed in what must have been less than a minute. Never did it so fast in my life. Then Hazor put a finger to his lips and motioned me to follow. In the hallway, instead of going toward the main stairs, he led the way to another door at the rear, and pushed it open. He snuffed out the candle, and in the dark, helped by only the palest wisp of clouded moonlight, we groped our way down a flight of rickety wooden stairs to the rock-strewn strip of land behind the inn. A few further cautious steps brought us to the water's edge, where a small boat was tied up.

Taking hold of the prow, Hazor motioned me to get in. Then he followed, gently shoved off, sat down and began pulling quietly at the oars. Ahead of us out on the lake, dotting the black expanse with flaring torches, I could see a dozen or more fishing boats, widely scattered.

"That one over there," Hazor said softly, pointing along the shore, "that's Peter."

I turned my head and saw the boat Hazor indicated, a brightly lit vessel a hundred yards or so from us. It was much larger than ours, and at bow and stern flaring torches stood upright, illuminating the boat's interior. So far as I could make out, there were six or seven men aboard.

"How do you know it's Peter?"

"Trailed him out last evening. Been fishing nearby ever since. Mostly we were out farther, but they had no luck. When they came in close like this and threw the nets I went for you."

"Glad you did, but have they—"

"Nothing big went overboard while I was watching. Can't tell what they might have with them in the boat besides the nets and the gear. Water's not very deep in here, so I'm sure they didn't do it while I was gone. And I can tell you that this is the first time they've been out on the lake since they got back."

It didn't seem the moment for questions, so we sat there in the dark ready to follow if they headed out. Only then did I begin to wonder what time it was, even what day. Being awakened like that,

I couldn't figure how long I'd been asleep, whether for minutes or hours. Shortly, my question was answered as a thin, grayish streak began to tint the darkness above the eastern shore.

"They're hauling the net," Hazor murmured, and he reached for an oar. A few minutes later the net was in, and Peter's boat started moving. But instead of heading out, it was pulling steadily for the land.

"See that little cove among the trees," said Hazor. "Probably going in there. Maybe stretch their legs and get some breakfast." Slipping an oar over the stern he started an easy sculling motion, and we began to drift in, paralleling Peter's boat.

A loud call from somewhere ashore broke the stillness and echoed dimly across the water. There were several words strung out, but all were muffled by distance. Almost immediately from the direction of Peter's boat, still moving and now only some hundred feet from land, came an answering shout. This time I thought I caught one word: "nothing." Again the voice from the shore called out, and once more the muffled string of words was lost on the air.

"Look," said Hazor, pointing at Peter's boat. "They've stopped and they're spreading the nets again."

"Quick, Hazor. Turn us round and make it seem as if we're leaving. Then let's go ashore where we can sneak up on that cove. I'm sure the voice came from in there."

The whole maneuver took about ten minutes, which in the circumstances seemed forever, but there was no way to do it faster without calling attention to ourselves. Hauling the boat up on the pebbly shore behind a screen of dense trees, we crept along carefully through the bushes and found a good hiding place behind some rocks topping a slight rise. Inching forward, we saw that below us was spread the little tree-ringed cove, its rim of beach sweeping around in a gentle curve. A few yards back from the water's edge, at about the center of the curve, a small fire reddened the dark sand. Beside the fire stood a hooded figure looking out over the water at Peter's boat, which was riding about where we'd left it. The figure, taking only a few steps this way or that to get a better view of the boat's activity, remained close to the fire, so we settled down to watch what developed. We hadn't long to wait.

Suddenly an excited shouting arose on the boat, several voices exclaiming loudly, and there was much scrambling movement among the men. I could see that they'd begun hauling the net, but were having trouble getting it in. Then the weirdest thing happened. One of the men jumped overboard, just stepped up on the side and leaped right over into the water, causing a great splash and leaving the boat rocking behind him. Then he began swimming into the cove. Almost at the same time, the other men gave up trying to haul the net aboard. Dragging it round to the stern, they hurriedly secured it, then came forward and bent over the oars. They were heading in too.

The swimmer entered shallow water, got to his feet and hurried up on the beach, his every step throwing a diminishing shower ahead of him. But he stumbled as he reached the fire and went down on his knees. The hooded man stretched out a hand and helped him up. I saw then, mainly from his unusual bulk, that the swimmer was Peter himself. After some brief words between the two, the other man threw back his hood. The hair was longish, but there wasn't enough light from the fire the way he was facing, and he stood just too far away for a good look.

The gliding boat crunched to a stop in the sandy shallows and six men jumped down from the bow, one after another. Quickly they walked toward the fire, where they crowded around Peter and the stranger. There was some talk, but all that reached our ears was a low mumble. Then Peter turned away, waded into the water beside the boat, unhooked the heavy net from the stern, took the ends over his shoulder and began dragging the whole thing up on the beach. It was a struggle even for him, and I began to think that there must be something besides a few fish in the folds, something about the size of a man's body. But as the net flattened out on the sand in the firelight, I saw that it was positively alive with big fish, writhing, hopping, glistening, a huge catch.

"That's why they couldn't get it aboard," Hazor whispered. "What a haul! Lucky the net didn't tear. I was thinking it wasn't only fish they had. The first cast in that same place came up empty. It's only fish, though."

For almost a half hour we crouched in nearly motionless suspense on our rocky perch, but nothing much happened. The whole bunch of them just lolled on the beach around the fire, cooking and eating fish and talking in muffled tones. It was only when I strained to stare a little harder at one of the men nearer the fire whose face was in our direction, his features lit by the glow, that I recognized another of the group. It was Thomas the Twin. I couldn't mistake that thin face and high hairline. Evidently, his disagreement with the others had not troubled their friendship.

Most of the time Peter and the stranger sat talking together a little off to the side. At one point, they stood up and strolled back toward the trees, still talking, and for some reason Peter became agitated. He stopped, faced the stranger and began gesturing vigorously. But it wasn't much of a disagreement. When another man from the group joined them, Peter quickly calmed down. Then all three turned and started back to the fire, walking straight toward us.

Suddenly it hit me, and I made a grab for Hazor's arm. "Take a good look at the stranger. Who does he remind you of?"

Hazor angled his hand in front of his eyes to block the fire's glare from his line of sight. "Can't say. Too far from the fire. They're still in shadow mostly."

"Look at his height compared to Peter, his general build. Look at that long hair. Is it the firelight or does the hair seem reddish, sort of coppery?"

"Sort of. Can't be sure from here. He's taller than Peter, well built but not so hefty. What about it?"

"Hazor, don't you understand?"

Staring down hard through the murky darkness, he made no reply. His slowness was exasperating. "Come on, Hazor! Doesn't he look like Jesus?"

"Like Jesus?" He turned to face me. "How do you mean?"

"A close resemblance, wouldn't you say?"

"Well, I don't know about——"

"Hazor, there's the man who appeared in the upper room!"

He looked back down at the beach and we both continued to stare, hoping that the stranger would come nearer the fire or might turn in a way that would light up his features. In a whisper Hazor asked, "Didn't you say that nobody could have fooled those men into thinking he was Jesus? Not if he stayed too long, you said, and let them get too close?"

"Yes, yes, I said that all right, and meant it. But that's a personal opinion. I may be overlooking something. We can't afford just to shut our minds, can we? Here's this hooded stranger, a look-alike, meeting with the Galileans at night in this deserted spot . . ."

"Wait a minute, sir. We still haven't had a good look at him. Lots of men are that height and that build. Anyway, I never saw Jesus up close myself. And if this man's your imposter, what's he doing here, parading around in the open, talking to everybody? That only gives them another chance to study his face. Couldn't get much closer than they are right now."

He was right, of course, and I fell silent as my initial excitement cooled. In my mind there arose the picture of the living Jesus and I saw him again in all his quiet power, so compelling. I'd been dead right the first time—nobody could impersonate him. Not this stranger, nobody. Getting a bit too anxious, I told myself, trying too hard.

Hazor leaned toward me. "Why don't we take them by surprise? Just walk right down there, tell them we've had them under official surveillance, ask why they left Jerusalem. Might catch them off guard."

I looked over at him. A bold stroke like that might work. If nothing else, at least we'd be able to identify the stranger and that in itself might get us somewhere. I turned the idea over in my mind to make sure it would not be a misstep, and was almost ready to move when something, I don't know what, an instinct, held me back. "No, Hazor, let's not give ourselves away yet. When they leave, if the stranger stays behind, I'll follow him. You take the boat and trail Peter."

Looking back down at the beach I saw that the men were now all up, crowding around the boat. Busily they were tossing the pile of fish aboard and folding the net. Yet something struck me as out of place. I counted the figures, then ran my eyes around the circle of trees hemming the cove. "Hazor, I don't see the stranger."

"I don't either, sir. How'd he get away so fast? Something's going on here. Maybe they suspected . . ."

"How could they? Look, there they go."

With Peter at the rudder and several men at the oars, the ponderous boat slipped steadily away from the beach. Quickly it glided from the cove, reached open water, then steered to the right along the tree-lined shore in the direction of Capernaum.

By now the sky, though still leaden, had brightened considerably. Soon it would be full daylight.

"I think there's no use following them," said Hazor. "If they had the body, they'd have dumped it last night. But I know they didn't. Now there's too much light to do it unless they head far out. Looks like they're going home."

My nerves were tingling, and for no good reason I could explain I felt like keeping up the chase in our own boat. At last I reluctantly agreed to call it off. Disappointed, vaguely resentful of having accomplished so little on our excursion, I rose stiffly to my feet and gratefully stretched my cramped limbs.

◆

T*HAT PESKY WOMAN*, the wife of the good Jacob, did not rest content with our conversation of the first day. At every opportunity she waylaid me, anxious to pour out Bethsaida's latest chatter about Jesus, or about any other topic that she thought might make an impression. So it was no surprise that it was she who brought me the first news of the strange rumor that Jesus had been seen alive.

It happened three days after our nocturnal outing on the lake. Hazor had returned to Capernaum to renew his watch on Peter's house, and I was still cooped up in my room, not even once going out for a breath of air. The hours dragged by at a turtle's pace but I used them to make some preliminary notes on our Galilean investigation and, that done, gave myself up to the scriptures. (It's surprising how much is said about the action of the wind, and whirlwinds, especially by the prophets. Yet I found that there's nothing quite like the way he used it the night of my visit, an interesting fact that confirms my impression of his strong originality. It's clear that he had the soul of a poet.)

Three days is an interminable amount of time to be pacing around a small room from bed to chair to window and then back again. I'd almost decided to take some direct action—what it might have been, the Lord only knows, perhaps confront Peter head-on—when the landlady came in with her news. Answering a knock at the door, I found her standing there, minus even the bowl of soup she usually brought up in the afternoon.

"Are you sure he's dead, sir? Jesus? Because either he is or he isn't, you know, and I've just come from three lady friends who say they saw him yesterday." She folded her hands on her apron, pursed her lips, and lifted her eyebrows, studying the effect of her announcement.

"Saw him?" I asked, sighing in mild despair. "Madam, you must understand that what you say is out of the question. I assure you the man is dead."

"Now, sir, I grew up with these ladies, right in this town. They're not the foolish sort. I told them what you said about him dying and being buried and all. They said they didn't care about that. They still said they saw him. And they heard him speak."

"Yes. I see. Well . . . look, I want to thank you very much for bringing me this interesting news. Curious, very curious. Thank you. Now I have some studying to—"

"Oh, if you'd just talk with them!"

"I'm sorry. I really can't spare the time to go tramping round Bethsaida. Perhaps tomorrow. Or the next day."

"But they're here, just downstairs! I brought them." Not waiting for a reply she hurried to the door, yanked it open, and was about to call out, when she gave a little start. Magically the three ladies had materialized in front of her. "I told you to wait below," she snapped in a whisper. Then she raised her voice and said pleasantly, "Come in, ladies, come in."

The three scurried through the door and stood in a line facing me. All were middle-aged and motherly, and all were wearing expectant smiles. I groaned. This little session threatened to occupy half an hour at least, and there appeared to be no way out without injuring the women's feelings and causing talk. Resigned, I smiled through the introductions, then invited my four guests to be seated. There were only three chairs, so the landlady said she'd stand. I took the bed and then we waited, the five of us looking blankly at each other.

"Well, *tell* him," urged the landlady. Promptly, all three of her friends began talking at once.

"Let's start with you," I said, pointing a finger at the one in the middle, who seemed the calmest.

"Yes, sir. You want to know if we saw the teacher, Jesus. We certainly did. Just as plain as you."

"Where did you see him?"

"The other side of Capernaum, near Gennesaret. That big hill with the bald side, just off the road where—"

"We were at a wedding," interrupted the florid-faced lady on the left, her tone a bit breathless, "my sister's boy. Coming back from it. Yesterday evening. And there they were, all those people going up the hill. We asked them and they said it was Jesus, said the teacher from Nazareth was up there. So we went too. Why, we thought he was dead, heard that he'd died in Jerusalem! But we saw him, so he didn't, did he?"

"How close were you?"

"Close enough. From here to there." She pointed across at an angle to the far corner of the room, about twenty feet from where she was sitting.

"How did you know it was Jesus? Ever see him before?"

"I should say! He used to come here to Bethsaida a lot, to visit the synagogue and just around. I saw him, oh, several times."

"Was his head uncovered?"

"Oh, yes. That nice, long, coppery hair."

"You heard him speak?"

"Yes, indeed. He spoke right out in that same way of his, so nice and all but still a bit, well, firm I suppose. And all the time more people were coming up."

"How many people would you say? As many as a dozen?" I must find a way to end this, I thought, and without giving offense or bringing on an argument over their honesty or eyesight. I could say that this new information was important, needed to be written down and sent to the council, and would they excuse me . . .

"They just kept coming and coming," answered the third woman. "By the time we left I guess there were hundreds on the hill, standing all around."

"Hundreds? Did you say hundreds?" The crudity of the woman's imagination disappointed me. I would have expected a touch more subtlety from such obvious gossips. "How many hundreds?"

The three looked at each other questioningly, the middle lady swiveling back and forth between the other two. Then she faced me and replied, "I'd say there were about six or seven hundred. Haven't seen that many in one place since Hillel's daughter's wedding. At least six."

This was really too much. Did they take me for a village idiot? "Ladies, you have indeed brought me important news. Now you must excuse me while I draft a memorandum of our little talk. Official report for the council, you know. Thank you very—"

"You'll want to write down my friends' names for your report," suggested the landlady, though her peremptory tone made it seem more like an order.

"Ah, yes, of course." I picked up the stylus and the wax tablet—papyrus and ink would have been wasted—and began writing as the ladies in turn called out their names and addresses. "There, now. That's all done."

"Don't you want the others?" asked the left-hand lady.

"Others?" I had a sudden nervous flash of myself sitting there hour after hour writing down hundreds of spurious names and addresses as the three informants spun out their fantasy.

"Naturally, we didn't know everybody. But I did notice two neighbors from Bethsaida, and there was another woman with her husband I know from Capernaum. My friends here saw people too."

When I'd done writing at the ladies' dictation, the list of names had grown to seventeen—friends, acquaintances, some cousins and uncles, a nephew, two sisters-in-law. Several were identified as from here in Bethsaida. The others came from half a dozen towns in the area, Chorazin, Gennesaret, Tiberias, Nain, so on. "Counting us, that makes twenty," said the middle lady, "and they'll all tell you the same thing."

No doubt they would, I thought to myself, if we could manage to find them in less than a month of slogging our way around the countryside. My respect for the women's inventive skill had been restored. "I shall be looking into the whole matter," I promised as I stood up and walked toward the door.

Shepherded by the landlady, expressing their respect for me and their gratitude for the interview, my three earnest informants glided from the room. I proffered a final word of thanks, giving a little wave as I shut the door behind them. Then, heaving a sigh of relief, I went over to the bed and sank wearily onto its miserably unyielding surface.

Something had better happen soon, I thought disgustedly.

As the heavy steps and babbling talk of the women faded down the stairs, I lay stretched on the bed, arms thrown out, eyes closed, my mind drifting . . . what would Sarah back in Jerusalem be doing now? Not easy to run our villa and its large staff, but she always keeps things up when I'm gone, which isn't often. We both like a well-run house because it's when things are under control and in some kind of order that you can afford to let up a bit now and then, something the young never seem able to grasp . . . what I wouldn't have given to have Sarah sitting right there with me to talk to at that moment . . .

Drowsiness was stealing over me when there came a knock at the door, a faint knock. (Let me say that I note this moment so deliberately because, looking back, I can see that in its quiet way it was the beginning of the change, and because even now I cannot predict the outcome.) At the knock I almost said aloud, oh no, not them again! Muttering to myself about the annoyance of busybody women, I rolled reluctantly off the bed and crossed the room.

Pulling the door open no more than a foot, I peered out. There in the hall stood Hazor, his face anxious. Quickly he slipped in, shut the door and turned to me. "I heard those women in here, sir, so I waited."

"Ah, Hazor, good to see you. Something's happened?"

"Yes, sir. Well, yes and no. I'm not sure." Searching through his pockets, he brought out a narrow roll of papyrus. "I don't know just how to put it. There's talk flying around Capernaum . . . people are saying, quite a lot of people are saying . . . well, that Jesus . . . was seen alive yesterday . . ."

"Hazor, you're not going to tell me that *you* saw him!"

"No, no, of course not. But what's going on? So many people in Capernaum claim they saw him. That's all anyone talks about."

"Relax, Hazor. I've just had a taste of that kind of nonsense myself. You saw those women."

That's not what I had meant to say. As the spoken words rose in my mind they were accompanied by a question I was trying not to ask myself. The words I did speak somehow slipped out almost of themselves, rushed out as if to veil the division in my thoughts. But then the smothered question forced itself on me: Bethsaida and Capernaum on the same day? Does empty-headed gossip travel so widely so fast?

"Tell me, Hazor, just what did you hear?"

"The talk is that Jesus was seen yesterday, out in the open, seen by hundreds of people. They saw him, heard him speak, spoke to him."

"Where?"

"On a hill near Gennesaret. I took the trouble to list some names. Didn't know what I was getting into. Most of these people I've spoken with personally." He unrolled the papyrus and let it dangle from his hand. The long sheet was crammed on both sides, column after column of names with addresses.

"Good Lord! How many?"

"A hundred and thirty-seven. With more time I might have gotten a lot more."

"You say you interviewed most of these?"

"Nearly a hundred, mostly in groups of two or three in and around Capernaum. Didn't take long. With the first dozen, maybe five minutes for each. As I went along, with everybody offering names of other witnesses, I spent less time questioning. It always came to the same thing: they knew Jesus from before, thought him a great teacher, maybe even a new prophet. Most had heard that he was in some kind of trouble in Jerusalem, but they were vague about it."

"Didn't they know he's been dead for over two weeks?"

"When I reminded them of the news—rumors, I put it—of his

death, most only shrugged. They'd laugh and say things like, 'Don't tell me what I saw with my own eyes. If that was a dead man I saw yesterday, I should be so dead!' No hesitation, no doubts."

"They all reacted like that?"

"Most did, but there were a few quieter ones, and they were weird. They'd look me in the eye and say right out that, yes, Jesus had died on the cross in Jerusalem. No arguments or excuses. Then with big smiles they'd say that death could not hold him. Funny the way they kept using those same words, death could not hold him. They wouldn't say anything else. Told me I should go talk to Peter. Simon Peter, they called him."

"Yes, of course. Peter again. More of that same fantastic stunt he pulled back home. That stranger on the beach . . ."

"A stunt, sir? You don't really think that Peter could have staged a thing like this, do you? Out in the open, with at least a hundred and thirty-seven witnesses?"

"A hundred and fifty-seven, unless you have duplicates. Maybe I don't. But what *are* we to believe?"

A sudden, sharp clatter answered my question as the wooden shutters on the tiny window began banging and rattling loudly, swung back and forth by a freshening breeze off the lake. At the sound my nerves jumped, and though I'd almost gotten used to the noise, I now found it vastly annoying. Picking up a towel, I went to the window. I was about to close it and stuff up the crack, just as I'd been doing every night since our arrival, when a strong gust whooshed past me into the room, ruffling clothes and tossing papers and books, and sending a small vase crashing noisily to the floor. Glancing at the scattered fragments and the bedraggled flowers, I found myself thinking that the wind blows where it wills, all right, and this time I certainly heard the sound of it. Aloud, I finished, "And I still don't know where it comes from or where it goes."

"Sorry?" inquired Hazor.

"Nothing. Just thinking." I closed the shutters and stuffed the towel between them. "So where does that leave us? Conspiracy? Mass hallucination again?"

Hazor went round picking up the books and papers, and several minutes passed before he spoke. "Probably three or four hundred people," he said suddenly, standing still in the middle of the room. "Some say five or more. Hardly a conspiracy with that many, I'd judge, though I'm no expert. Could you have hallucination with that many, in broad daylight? Most of these witnesses don't believe Jesus died to start with, the ones I talked to. All they're claiming, most of them, is that yesterday they saw a certain man that they'd met several times before. Nothing there that I can see to cause hallucination."

He paused, went to a chair by the far wall and slumped down on it, his long legs straight out, his chin on his chest. Then he shoved himself up straight, and opened his mouth as if to speak. But he changed his mind and his gaze dropped back to the floor.

"Well, go on," I invited. "What else?"

"Nothing, only I was wondering . . . I mean, what do you think? Could it be just barely poss—"

"Don't even say it!" I cut him off sharply. "Get a grip on yourself, man!" I went to the bed and sat down heavily. "You've been talking with too many of these simpletons."

Momentarily, he looked pained. Then he grinned. ". . . possible that the body you put into the tomb wasn't really dead. Still had a spark of life."

For some reason the suggestion didn't startle me as it might have. Naturally it was out of the question, but all I managed to think of in response was a cool, "And then?"

"Just for the sake of argument—if he wasn't dead, couldn't he have been taken from the tomb by his friends, patched up, and then, well, sort of put on display?"

"Forget it, Hazor. Even for the sake of argument, it's silly. Say he wasn't quite dead. I can tell you he couldn't have been far from it, within an inch. Nobody could have patched him up that fast, so he was able to stand and talk to crowds of people. Forget it."

"Don't know, sir. But still it's worth—"

"Beaten mercilessly with sticks and whips, flogged with that deadly flagrum, his skull a mass of punctures, nailed hand and foot to a cross, lanced in the side, hour after hour of the most awful agony—ah, Hazor, you didn't see him, the pity of it. I know what death looks like, I've faced it before. It's ridiculous even to—"

There was a knock at the door and the landlady's head popped in. "Message for you, sir," she said as she came toward me waving a folded piece of papyrus. "Now, who's this from?" I muttered as I took it, not concealing my annoyance at the interruption. Undoing the fold I read:

> *Simon Peter to the worthy Nicodemus, greeting:*
> For several days now we have been looking forward to the pleasure of a visit from you. There is much to talk of, especially after what took place yesterday, about which I know you have heard. Please come to see us when it is convenient for you, but the sooner the better. Your man who has been so diligently watching my house can show you where I live. Please tell him he is also very welcome to come inside. Peace to you in Christ Jesus.

That's that, I sighed to myself, getting up and handing the note to Hazor. No sense in hiding any longer if Peter knew all about us. Must have his own efficient little network. Well, at least I was freed from this prison of a room.

Christ Jesus, no less. So Peter has decided to get back into the Messiah business. I should have guessed.

◆

SHE REMINDS ME very much of Sarah, Peter's wife does. Of course she's many years younger and of a commoner background. But there's that same gentle air of patience mixed with strong good sense, and a way of making you think that she knows a good deal more than she lets on. Also like Sarah, with a minimum of fuss she soon has you feeling at home. She and Peter welcomed us graciously and throughout the visit he made no mention of the unpleasantness at our last meeting. To keep things calm I took the cue.

Particularly I had decided that I would not raise the matter of his possession of the bloodstained cloth. It was still strong evidence against him, but dwelling on it might only defeat my purpose in coming here. I even cautioned Hazor not to mention it. So when Peter himself casually brought it up, I was barely able to hide my surprise. The cloth was safely stored away in a cupboard, he said as he led us inside. "Would you like to see it again? It's no trouble."

"No, no," I replied in some discomfort, "that won't be necessary. But thank you."

His house isn't large, only two or three tiny rooms that I could see, with a few nooks and crannies adding to the space. But even with the overflow of fishing gear thrown into corners and dangling from the walls, it's all kept neat and comfortable. We had complete privacy for our talk, which took place in a back room at a small, roughly made table (one of the table's legs was wobbly and out of line and as we took our chairs Peter gave it a little kick to straighten it, saying he'd fix it tomorrow. I had to smile at the way his wife, who was just leaving us, lifted her eyes at that).

Much of what was said between us repeated the substance of what I've already set down, so I need not give our talk in detail. There was one new thing, however, and it caught me unawares. Without a blink he actually insisted that most—or is it all?—of the prophets from Samuel onward "proclaimed this day," to give his own words. Then he reeled off a string of citations to show how Jesus was—is—the Messiah, and he soberly declared that the "precious blood of Christ" was offered as some sort of "ransom." He has even dug up several passages that, believe it or not, he links to the crucifixion itself. There's a line in the Psalms, "Not a bone of him shall be broken," which he connects with the soldiers not bothering to break the legs. Then Zechariah has, "They shall look on him whom they have pierced." The nails, of course, and the spear thrust. Another line he gives from the Psalms nicely matches that disgusting scene I witnessed myself, the greedy soldiers haggling over the clothes: "They parted my garments among them, and for my clothing they cast lots."

All very neat, all very ingenious on Peter's part. At least it speaks well for his industry in poring over the holy pages. But he's really quite in earnest, that's the pathetic thing.

Our main topic was that business on the hill near Gennesaret, and this we covered at some length. The number of people present that day who saw and heard Jesus, he claims, was in excess of five hundred, and he offered to have me talk to many of them—he couldn't resist adding with a wry smile, "I mean people besides those your efficient helper has already tracked down." I conceded the point that there had been a large crowd on the hill, and I suggested we set that question aside just then. I'll copy here a sampling from my original hasty notes of the discussion that followed. It shows what I'm up against with this man.

I said there was one very simple and obvious way that the whole matter, once and for all, could be settled. Just take me to see Jesus, let me talk to him. Where was Jesus now, at that moment?

He didn't know.

I asked when Jesus would return or be available again.

He didn't know.

I asked how many times he'd seen and talked to Jesus since the tomb was found to be empty.

He thought and then said five.

I asked where Jesus stayed or kept himself in between each of those five appearances.

He didn't know.

I asked why this resurrected Jesus found it necessary to remain in hiding. Only a few hours of his time could be accounted for in the space of three weeks. Even his friends seemed ignorant of his whereabouts.

He said it wasn't a matter of hiding. But he said he had to confess that he didn't know, not with certainty.

I asked why he understood so little about matters that apparently were of great importance to him.

He said that it wasn't his place to demand answers. In Jesus' own good time he would know all, or so much as Jesus might choose to reveal.

I asked if he could tell me whether Jesus had disclosed any of his plans for the future, and what were they.

He said not entirely—but then he went on to announce that Jesus would soon leave the earth and ascend to heaven! Just like that! Not a trace of hesitation or discomfort or apology as he said it. Not a trace!

I asked how Jesus in that case could fulfill his role as Messiah. Didn't we have to see him, talk to him, if he wanted us to admit that he had risen from the grave? Why not go around the country showing himself to people? Why not set up a headquarters somewhere, and let people come to him?

He said no, peoples' minds weren't made like that. Most wouldn't believe even then. They'd just say that he had never died to start with. Only the witnesses who'd been with Jesus all along, those who saw him die, were entitled to evidence and proof. For others it had to depend on faith. How else could you expect people a hundred or a thousand or two thousand years from now to believe? "If five hundred witnesses are not sufficient to convince you today," he finished quietly, "will five thousand be enough to convince the next generation? Will it take fifty thousand to impress people a century from now?"

The mention of a thousand years was made so casually that it took my breath away—here was no petty scheming of wily rustics, this was hoaxing on the grand scale! "What faith is it," I replied in some agitation, "which seeks to convince people about a stupendous event like this, yet which no responsible persons have seen or verified?"

His answer was so prompt, and for the moment seemed so apt and forceful, that I almost questioned whether the thought was original with him. I give it here very much in his own words.

"Everything we have accomplished in God," he said with a shrug of his burly shoulders, "has been done first by faith. Surely, Nicodemus, as a teacher in Israel, you know this? Noah by faith built the ark, didn't he, because he believed in the reality of an event as yet unseen? Abraham heard God's call and went out by faith, didn't he, not even knowing where he was to go? Moses by faith saved the remnant out of Egypt, taking them through the parted sea as if on dry land. Joshua by faith crumpled the stout walls of Jericho, and wasn't it by faith that Daniel stopped the mouths of the lions and came out of the den? Gideon, Samson, David, Samuel—and how many others!—all these prospered in God by faith, and I tell you that without faith no man can prosper in God or please him. You ask what faith is this?"

He paused, then with both elbows resting on the table and his large hands giving emphasis to his words, he finished offhandedly, as if he were stating a simple fact, "It is the assurance of things hoped for, the conviction of things not seen."

About now, Peter's good wife came along and said we had been talking long enough, that we should stop for a while to have some lunch. I wasn't hungry but I was very glad of the interruption, for my annoyance at Peter's naive complacency was growing fast. Where's the use of talking seriously to a man whose mind works like this?

The visit did have its one decidedly jarring moment, and it has left its mark. As Hazor and I were taking our leave, outside the door I stopped long enough to ask about those five occasions on which Peter claimed to have met Jesus. There'd been two encounters in Jerusalem, supposedly, and there was this latest appearance to the five hundred, but that made only three. He explained that back in Jerusalem there'd been a third meeting, a week after the first two. And up here in Galilee there'd been a second.

"Oh? When did the other one happen?"

"Several nights ago, on the shore near Bethsaida."

"Near Bethsaida?"

"There's a small cove along in there. We'd been fishing all night without taking much. Didn't want to go home with an empty bottom, so we tried the shallows. Jesus was on the shore and he called to us. I got so worked up when I understood who it was, I jumped from the boat and swam in!" Laughing at the memory of his own exuberance, he finished, "I get carried away sometimes. Well, why not, sometimes?"

He fell silent and his gaze dropped pensively to the ground. When he spoke again, his voice was restrained. "For me it was the most important meeting of all, and I only pray that I'll be equal to the task, that I can carry the burden. . . . Thirty or forty years, and then . . ." A vague shudder passed over his large frame, and for a moment his frank face took on a distant look. Then his manner brightened again and he added, "I'm very glad you and your friend came to visit. We'll have to talk more another time."

Walking down to the boat, Hazor and I were both sunk in a brooding silence, both of us apparently occupied by the same thought. He was the first to voice it, but not until after we'd reached the wharf, gotten into the boat and were well out on the water. Looking more and more puzzled, he suddenly stopped rowing and leaned forward on the oars. Staring straight at me he said, "Peter couldn't have known we were watching him in the cove that night. What would he gain by lying to us about it?"

My answer was a grunt.

"He could have invented any old sensational story, but this was pretty tame. And it was the truth. It did happen that way, and he did meet someone."

I grunted again, and for long moments we both sat motionless and unspeaking, letting the boat drift. Across the calm surface in the cool evening air it glided, slowly and steadily, serenely propelled by the light winds. What Hazor said next was about what I expected him to say. "All I mean, sir, is that it *could* have happened. Some life left in him. Rescued by his friends. That would explain practically everything."

"I know, I know. But I'm saying that it *didn't* happen. How could it? Good Lord, Hazor, I *held* that bloody corpse in my own arms! Anyway, you're overlooking something. Say some life remained in the body. How could Peter have known? Of course he couldn't. Why then, in your theory, would he steal the body? No, it doesn't hang together. And please, *don't* suggest that in some mysterious fashion he could have revived by himself in the tomb and made his own way out. It would take a magician to move that stone from inside."

"Well . . . not really, you know." He was looking down between his feet in moody abstraction.

"What?"

"Moving the stone from the inside. I mean that would be easy, no trouble at all."

That did stop me. "And just how . . ."

"Topple it. Push the top of the stone straight out, away from the wall. Just shove it over." With a tinge of smugness in his voice he added, "These closure stones aren't designed to prevent a tomb's *occupants* from getting out."

His solemn air in focusing on that isolated aspect of the question I found amusing in its sudden youthful earnestness. I was about to list the obvious difficulties when he added, sounding a bit defensive, "Oh, I'm not suggesting that it happened like that. Just saying it wouldn't be hard to do. But of course when the falling stone smacked the ground in the vestibule there'd be a tremendous noise and the guards were nearby and even if they were sleeping they—"

"Not to mention that you're assuming an astounding recovery for the sealed-in victim, a half-dead man having the strength to knock over that heavy stone. How much did you estimate it weighed?"

"I said I wasn't sugg . . . sixteen hundred pounds."

"Let's see. How much of those sixteen hundred pounds would the victim have to move in order to topple the stone? Half? A third? Let's say a quarter. Four hundred pounds. Or even say three, if you like. I have only average strength for my age and build, but I must be a lot stronger than a dying man who has suffered a serious blood loss. I wonder if I could budge three hundred pounds in a situation like that. Remember, because of the low doorway the top of the stone couldn't be reached from inside. The shove would have to be exerted practically at the stone's center."

With the index finger of his right hand Hazor began tracing imaginary numbers on the open palm of his left hand. He seemed in absolute earnest.

"Never mind that, Hazor. Let's go a step further. Say the impossible did happen. Say the victim somehow revived and then managed, somehow, to get out of the tomb, somehow elude the guards and somehow get away. Now we have the spectacle of a naked, bloody apparition staggering along the road and stumbling up to the city gate. Not your common, everyday sight. Not your ordinary traveler seeking a night's lodging."

"All right, sir, all right. Forget all that. Go back to what we were saying about his friends. Why couldn't they have gone to the tomb to steal the *dead* body, only to find when they got there that he *wasn't* dead? And since we're theorizing . . . no, never mind." He sat up straight, grasped the oars and began a slow pulling. I could see by the cross look on his face that he'd been stung by my answer. I could also see that his own unspoken thought was still prodding him.

"Come on, Hazor, what were you going to say?"

He stopped rowing, angled the oars inboard and leaned forward again, his eyes defiant. "Well, I mean if these Galileans are as slippery as you say, maybe they *did* know he wasn't dead. Maybe they planned it that way. You said yourself that Jesus surprised everyone by dying so quickly, that he spent only a few hours on the cross when they thought he might last a day or two. And didn't somebody lift him a drink just before the end? Who's to say there wasn't some kind of drug in it, something to put him out, make it look as if he'd died?"

By the way his eyebrows lifted I knew that he was more than half serious, carried away by the fascination of the problem. It took me a second or two to recover from the novel suggestion. "My God, Hazor, there are times when you show cunning worthy of the noble Romans themselves! What kind of drug? You can't just say drug, and let it go at that. How was it smuggled into the pail of vinegar wine—which by the way was on hand for the soldiers themselves to drink while they waited, not for the dying. You didn't know that? It's true. These Roman thugs, you seriously think they can't tell the difference between a drug stupor and death? They've had lots of poor victims faint on the cross, you know, but that doesn't fool them. They know death. Oh, don't they know death! What about the spear? It sank into his side at least the length of my hand. I *saw* it go in. I *saw* the blood gush out. His insides must have been all ripped up, even the heart."

"Wait a minute, sir. Supposing that the—"

"When would his friends have conceived this plan to drug him? Not until sentence of death had been passed, of course. But that gave them only a few hours. Not much time to get things ready. Then there's the burial, they'd have to manage that part, too, wouldn't they—where, and how, and so on—so he could be rescued. It was Joseph's tomb, you know. Shall we say that Joseph was part of the plot?"

Now feeling thoroughly worked up, I paused in my recital of objections only long enough to take a breath, then I went racing on. "Maybe we can go further. Maybe Jesus himself was in on the scheme, maybe *he* planned the whole thing, crucifixion and drugs and all, so he could amaze us by returning to life. If we're dreaming up plots about drugs and reviving half-dead bodies, then any crazy notion will do, the weirder the better. Who needs evidence? Or logic. Well, yes, we'd have to explain how a high-minded, wonder-working prophet, a spiritual genius, suddenly became a charlatan or a madman—"

"Excuse me, sir," Hazor interrupted as he lifted his eyes and gazed anxiously around. "It's clouding over fast. And the wind's from the north, blowing us out. Better think about getting back in."

Only then did I realize how dark the day had grown, and looking up I was startled to discover the sky so low, with masses of ugly black clouds moving ponderously down from the north. And we were nowhere near land. Lost in talk, propelled by the deceptively slight breeze, we had quietly drifted to the southwest, away from Bethsaida. We should have been hugging the shore, but were at least a mile out.

"Looks bad, Hazor, but maybe it'll blow over."

"I've heard about the squalls on this lake, sir. The wind comes blasting over those high hills above the town there, then drops on the water like an avalanche. Capsize a boat in minutes, they say." He was now tugging strongly at the oars, but the water had begun to roughen and the land seemed to come no closer.

Rapidly unfolding from within their own murky depths, the angry clouds prodigiously blossomed until they seemed to overspread the whole surface of the lake. Hanging low, they cast over sky and water a deadening pall of shadow and gloom, and in no time at all the shorelines were blotted out. With increasing force the furious wind swept down on us, roiling the dark surface of the tossing water. Soon violent, contrary waves, booming and crashing heavily against the boat, began pounding us from every side. Rain, falling in big drops, came at us driven in sheets by the howling wind.

Blinded and drenched by the downpour, deafened by the roaring gale, Hazor and I clung with all our strength to the boat's wildly tossing sides. In my worst dreams I had never imagined myself in a scene of such raging chaos, helpless before what seemed all the malevolent forces of nature released against us in a single massive stroke. That it could have happened so fast seemed impossible.

Hazor's voice called faintly. Shielding my eyes from the pelting rain, I looked up. "Lie down in the bottom," he was shouting, pumping his hand up and down. Even as he spoke, the bow jerked skyward, climbing a high wave. Immediately another huge swell broke over us, and I watched in shock as Hazor was lifted bodily on the crest of the pouring flood. Arms and legs flailing, he was carried overboard.

I shoved myself toward him along the side of the heaving boat, reaching out as far as I could. But I was promptly flung down, getting a hard bang on the head and hurting my wrist. I struggled up and tried again. This time the boat dipped violently over another foaming crest, and in an instant it was yanked from under me. For long moments I seemed actually to hang suspended in the air. Then I tumbled down into the lake's writhing surface, thrashing and gasping. In utter panic I gulped for breath, but water flooded into my mouth and throat instead—and from that point I remember no more of the storm.

No matter how I persist in analyzing what happened that day, I can't understand it. I go over everything step-by-step and second-by-second, but am unable to isolate or define the critical moment, the transition between that awful instant when I thought I was drowning, and finding myself rescued and safe. When next I was aware of anything, I was sitting in the boat within a few yards of the Bethsaida shore, and the storm was over. The clouds had disappeared, the wind had died away, the calm of evening had returned. And at the opposite end of the boat, in the bow, sat Hazor.

In a confused stupor we stared at each other. Neither, apparently, was badly injured. At last I managed to ask weakly, "How did you do it? How did you get back?"

With an effort he turned his head and threw a glance at our inn, which stood on the shore a short distance away. Then he gazed up for a long moment at the bright, blue sky. Finally he turned back to me. "I thought it was you."

Like myself, he could recall nothing that had happened after those appalling seconds we spent struggling in the water. Nor, just yet, could we bring ourselves to move. So we sat there trading opinions on what had happened, how we'd gotten back to the boat, how the boat had come to shore. The only possible answer, we agreed, was that we'd both been thrown back in by the leaping waves, just as we'd been thrown out. We also agreed that the storm must have ended very suddenly, at about the same time we were washed over, blown itself out as these Galilean squalls do. The wind could then have shifted around and driven us north to the land. Only then did I notice something else, that my clothes were perfectly dry. Feeling for dampness in my arms and legs, I asked in surprise, "Hazor, are your clothes wet or dry?"

His hands went to the material on stomach and arms, then dropped to his thighs. "Dry," he replied in a puzzled tone, "all dry." We must have been sitting there half-dazed, I thought, much longer than I had at first imagined. How long would that have been?

Nursing our bruises we walked slowly back to the inn, staying along the shoreline so as not to encounter anyone who might be in a mood for conversation. Over and over as we went I repeated to myself how very odd it was that neither of us could remember what had happened out there on the lake. It would come to me later, I decided at last. Meantime, in my heart I did not forget to whisper a fervent Thank God.

◆

S*HE OPENED THE DOOR WIDE* at my knock, then stood there wearing a pleasantly inquiring look on her face that said, Whoever you are, welcome.

I'd never met her before, yet I knew her on the instant. No mother and son could be more alike. But what struck you in him as force and authority, in her somehow softened into tenderness and a delicate kind of warmth. Like him, she was rather tall, nearly my own height, and gracefully formed. Her unlined face and glowing skin gave her a youthful air, though I'm sure she must have been nearing fifty. I had not expected her to be here, and now, standing at the door, I felt unaccountably flustered to have her calm eyes meet mine so unwaveringly.

"Good morning, sir," she greeted easily, her voice soft and low, "the ladies are all here waiting for you."

Her manner and attitude were not those of a mourner, I noted in some slight surprise. A brave woman, in full possession of herself. Not hard to see where her son's wonderful strength of character had come from.

She stepped aside, invited me in, then led the way along a central hallway to large double doors at the rear. As we entered the tastefully furnished parlor, all six women rose to their feet and Mary took care of the introductions. To Joanna and Magdalene I said how glad I was to see them again, and looking so well. The others were new to me. There was Salome, mother of young John and mistress of this house. There was another woman named Mary, an aunt of Jesus, I think she said. And there was a widow named Hannah with her daughter Abigail, a young woman so small and thin it didn't seem she could belong to the heavy, large-boned woman beside her.

This gathering had been arranged by Peter, at my request, so that I could interrogate the women who'd been at the tomb that morning. He'd been very good about it, setting no conditions, even suggesting that the meeting take place at John's house, which was larger and more convenient for all. Nor did he ask what I meant to discuss, although I did explain to him that I wanted to straighten out the facts and the timing of all those comings and goings. When he acts helpful like this it's hard to see him as a manipulator. Of course it only means that he has managed to stay one jump ahead of me. Well that, I told myself, was about to change.

On greeting me, Salome felt it necessary to apologize for her husband's absence from the house, which led to a strangely unpleasant and slightly embarrassing moment for me. He was now running three boats of his own, she said, and there had been unusually big shoals of fish in the waters near Tiberias. Otherwise he would have been there to welcome me himself. "These days the fish see more of him than I do," she finished with a laugh.

"Your son John must be with him," I suggested. "I imagine it isn't easy to get good help when the whole fleet is on the go." It was a casual remark meant to relax the atmosphere before we started, but instead it uncovered a strain in Salome's family.

In a rather sad tone she answered, "No, he's not. James, either—I have two sons, you know. They spend all their time at Peter's house now." As she went on, her manner became earnest and confiding, as if telling me about it made a difference. I tried not to let my discomfort show.

"Their father can't understand why they don't help on the boats. His own sons. He taught them all he knows and he says they're almost as good at it as he is. When they were boys they loved to be out on the water, oh they couldn't wait for each morning. Now they say there are more important things, and then it's an argument and he says they're not children anymore, and shouldn't they help put bread on the table, and my sons get excited and their father gets hurt and . . . it's very unpleasant." She lifted her hands helplessly, shook her head and gave a long, heavy sigh. "Of course we know that things can't be the same anymore. But their poor father, he works so hard. All he ever wanted was to have his sons working beside him. And he does need help. Oh, I can see his side, too, and I just don't know."

How many times I'd heard this same lament from other parents over their sons, and in matters far less compelling. Still, it is always a little sad to hear it and I tried to sound encouraging without getting too involved. "I have no sons—two daughters—but I know how your husband must feel. Well, your boys are young. I'm sure they'll come down to earth once this thing"—I caught myself in time, no need to antagonize—"once they see they can do both. A few days spent fishing with their father, then a few days going round with Peter. That would suit you, wouldn't it?"

"If only!"

I walked to the chair indicated by Salome and sat down. Mary excused herself and left the room, saying she'd be in the kitchen if needed.

The six seated women were ranged around me more or less in a semicircle, waiting for me to begin. It was then I realized that, stupidly, I hadn't prepared a list of specific questions, hadn't given enough thought to the best way of approaching this. As I looked at each of the women in turn—their inquisitive faces showing an eagerness to cooperate, for which I was grateful—I understood for the first time how very subtle was the task of delving into people's memories. You couldn't do it roughly, abruptly, like shoveling down through layers in the earth. Perhaps it was a bit like lowering a net for fish—you had to know just how, just where, and just when, or you'd probably come up with an empty net. The fish that swim in the memory I'm sure must be as slippery as those in the lake.

"Magdalene, I'll begin with you, if I may. Now I'll ask you to think back carefully to that morning at the tomb, your first visit. You're walking with the other women. They stop to buy the spices, and you go on alone. It's still very early. Take a moment and think back. Close your eyes if you like—good, that will help you concentrate. See yourself walking rapidly along the road, that long, dusty road, then turning in at Golgotha. All right, now, you're coming up to the tomb, approaching the vestibule. Stop there and in your imagination look up. Do you see any light in the sky?"

"It was dark," she said without hesitation, her eyes still closed. "I don't remember any light."

"Picture the scene to yourself. Look around in it. Is there any sign of other people there at that moment? Not just at the tomb, anywhere nearby. Someone moving around the base of the hill, maybe higher up. Or among the trees. A sound. Anything."

"No, nothing."

Her reply had come a little too quickly. "Now, Magdalene, certainly you were upset, nervous. That could have blurred your attention. Maybe there's a dim memory lurking at the back of your mind. Just relax and in your mind's eye put yourself back at Golgotha."

She opened her eyes. "That's *how* I know, sir. Because I *was* upset and frightened, especially when I looked inside and found the body was gone. I did look around and listen. I felt there might be something. But no. Then I ran."

"All right. Thank you." I turned to Joanna.

"Now, Joanna, you said that you and the others came along, what was it, about ten minutes after Magdalene?"

"About that, sir."

"I'll ask you to do the same thing—shut your eyes then stop and think a moment and get a picture of your little group as it arrives at Golgotha, silently hurrying along. Some of you are ahead, some of you back a ways. Now you're approaching the vestibule of the tomb. All right now, try and recall, is it still quite dark? Any hint of first light?"

"Yes, all dark. Well, I think so, I mean I wasn't specially watching. But if you ask—"

Salome interrupted. "Excuse me, Joanna. I think you must mean that it was dark when we *started* from the house to go to the tomb. We did start before sunup. But you remember we went into that old woman's place by the gate to buy the spices and had to get her out of bed? And of course walking took time. When we reached Golgotha I'm sure there was the tiniest streak of light just showing over Olivet."

Joanna, her eyes open, looked doubtful. "I suppose. But it was still very dark when we got there. In the tomb Hannah had to light her little torch."

"Now Joanna, Salome, did either of you see or hear anyone in the vicinity, I mean besides that young man in the white robe?"

"*Two* young men in white," the ample Hannah broke in emphatically. "There were two, not one."

"Two?"

Gently she poked her daughter with a hefty elbow. "Weren't there two, Abbie? You saw them." Before the daughter could respond, Hannah turned back to me and added, "You can ask Salome and Mary there. Two young men."

"Yes, sir," said Joanna, "there were two. That's what Mary and Hannah told us later. I saw only the outside one."

Mary and Abbie were both nodding yes.

I turned to Magdalene. "And you?"

"Not the first time, but the second. When I went back there were two men sitting inside."

"Yes, now I recall you telling that to Peter."

Hannah spoke again, her tone insistent. "Ladies, ladies, why keep saying men? We know they were angels. Then say so. They were two *angels*." She pronounced the word with emphasis, then clasped her hands in her lap, stiff-armed, hunched her shoulders and waited for my reaction.

Controlling myself, I glanced round at the others. All five were looking directly at me and nodding their heads in agreement. "Angels? How do you know? What do angels look like?"

Softly, her earnest tone full of sincerity, Salome answered, "We just know they were. I guess when you meet an angel you don't have to be told. There's something different about them, a brightness. You feel it. Their eyes. One was outside, standing in the vestibule, one was inside. The inside one spoke to us. Even from what he said we know he was an angel."

"What did he say?"

Salome looked at Hannah. "You tell."

Inching forward in her chair, Hannah planted her hands firmly on her plump knees. "Sir, you may believe as you like. But the angel did speak to us, and here's what he said. 'Why look for the living among the dead? Jesus is risen, he's not here. See the place where they laid him.' Then he told us we must go tell Peter."

I looked slowly round the circle, letting my gaze rest momentarily on the face of each of the women—all were dead serious, no doubt of it. Now what sort of question, I asked myself in some discomfort, is proper in a situation like this? I'd never met anyone before who claimed to have had the privilege of standing eye-to-eye with an angel! And here they reported it as if they'd just run into an old neighbor. Marvelous! Do you ask how tall the angels were, whether fat or thin, what dialect they spoke? And didn't some of them have wings? That would have been a good touch.

"Let me ask how many of you went inside, into the chamber."

"Mary and me and Abbie," Hannah replied. "Joanna and Salome were back a ways. I think they didn't go in—did you?—or maybe Salome went in after us. Hard to remember."

The shy Abigail, who hadn't spoken to then, now broke in, her voice hushed and breathless. "We all looked, but the body wasn't there. Nothing was there except the cloth and we looked all around but the body wasn't anywhere, not in the other niches or anywhere.

And then we ran. I ran first." Her voice trailed to a halt as her mother patted her hand approvingly.

"Thank you, Abbie," I said, then looked round at the others. "Now the man on the outside—sorry, the angel—did he say anything? Did he do anything?"

The words "yes" and "no" blended in a chorus, and the women began arguing among themselves, some insisting that the outside man had spoken, some that he hadn't. This was getting us nowhere. "All right, ladies. Now tell me, how long would you say you remained at the tomb before running off? From what you've said, it seems hardly three or four minutes."

"Not that long," Salome responded. "To me it's all a blur, but I think even three minutes is too much."

"And which way did you run after . . ." I stopped suddenly as a word Abigail had used echoed at the back of my mind. I turned to her. "Abigail, did you say cloth? You saw a *cloth* in the tomb?"

She shrank back a little in her chair. "Yes, sir. Oh, but we didn't touch it. We left it just as it was."

"What kind of cloth do you mean?"

"That same long one, the linen one you and Joseph wrapped the body with. It was lying there."

"You saw *that* cloth, the burial shroud?"

"Why, yes, sir."

"Listen! I want you to describe what it looked like. Think back carefully. Tell me how it was lying, exactly *where* it was!"

Unnerved a bit by my insistent tone, the girl shrank back and leaned toward her mother, who responded to the silent plea. "Now, sir, you mustn't keep at Abbie like that. She saw the cloth, all right, we all did. It was on the stone ledge, stretched out. The ledge to the right as you enter."

"Entirely flat or rumpled or thrown about—what?"

"Flat. Nice and flat. Smooth."

"The top half, do you recall if that was flat, too, laid flat over the bottom half?"

"Oh, I did notice that. The top half was thrown up at the head, I mean where the head was. Not rolled, you know, more as if it had been picked up and then just dropped. Some little cloths were on the other side of the long one, by themselves."

Our session lasted for another half hour, but nothing further was developed about the cloth—which the women insisted they left on the bench untouched—or about anything else. Frustratingly, there was no clue at all as to the possible identity of the "angels." At one point I ventured to suggest that, rather than heavenly visitors, the two might in reality have been the gardener and his helper—Salome had already sent for those men, I reminded the ladies. But this idea was roundly rejected by all six women at once: yes they *were* frightened, and yes the light *was* bad, but they weren't dolts, they insisted icily, did I think they were dolts—they'd *have* to be dolts to mistake men for angels!

Hannah asked rather haughtily whether I believed in angels, that is, angels as messengers of God. When I said of course I did, in general, she lifted her eyebrows and tilted her head back as if to say, Then how do you know that *these* weren't angels? Just then I could think of nothing in rebuttal that might have seemed adequate.

In any case, my thoughts had become fixed on that cloth. If the women were telling the truth, if they'd actually seen the cloth in the tomb, it made all the difference. It meant that Peter could be telling the truth about finding it there when he and John paid their own hurried visit later. In that event, possession of the cloth proved little or nothing.

But could Peter and John have gone twice to the tomb—once to steal the body, and later to retrieve the cloth?

Why not take it the first time?

Why go back for it?

Why take it at all?

◆

THE REAR PORTION of my skull had begun throbbing, which always happens when I skip meals or try to eat on the run. But eager as I was to get back to the inn for a hot dinner and a nap, after leaving the women I decided to delay my departure from John's house to have one final interview. It proved to be worthwhile, even fascinating, but in a way I now wish that I had gone straight home. Some things are better left undisturbed.

As Salome walked me to the door, on the spur of the moment I asked, "Do you think Mary would talk to me, just briefly?" From seeing his mother as I entered the house, how well she was bearing up, I thought that a short conversation about her son might not be too painful for her. And I did have a real curiosity to know something of his background. "Of course, if she'd rather not . . ."

"I'm sure she wouldn't mind. Let's see if she's still in the kitchen."

At a long, narrow table in the kitchen's center, its surface strewn with heaps of vegetables, Mary sat alone busily shredding cabbage. When Salome explained what I wanted, she smiled her agreement, laid down the knife, went for a chair, and invited me to join her at the table. "You won't care if I go on with this?" she asked. "They let me do nothing here, say it isn't right for me now. But you know I kept house for thirty years and it's hard to sit still. You'd think after I'd raised six children I'd welcome a rest! But I can't find half enough to keep me busy."

"A nice size family," I said, sitting down. "How many boys?"

"Four all together, and two girls."

"I suppose Jesus was the eldest of the brothers?"

"Yes, he was."

"With that many in the house I guess it's safe to say that Jesus as a youngster wasn't spoiled! How did he get along with the others?"

"Really very well. They all just seemed to troop after him as the leader. But they weren't all mine," she finished with a laugh. "I had only one. The others were children of my sister-in-law. They'd been left orphans very young and they came to live with us. They're all grown now but they're still just like my own."

As we talked I was trying to decide how to get the conversation started on the track I wanted. I could hardly come right out and ask if she believed that her dead son had come back to life. I couldn't ask point-blank if she had seen him, talked to him. I'll inquire about her husband, I thought—I didn't even know his name—but it was she who spoke first. Pausing in her work, she glanced casually up from the cabbage under her hands. "Please, you mustn't be uncomfortable with me. Yes, I have met my son since his resurrection. We talked for a long while."

She said it so simply, and with such a look of easy, charming sincerity on her smiling face, that it seemed she must really believe what she said. I let several seconds pass in silence as I groped for a question and a tone of voice which would be properly respectful and which would not too blatantly betray my own feelings. "May I ask when this was?"

"The Sunday he rose. Long before dawn."

"You must have been the first to see him, the first to know what had happened. You knew about his"—I hoped she didn't spot my hesitation over the word—"resurrection before any of the others?"

"Yes."

"Where were you at the time?"

"In my room at the big house in Jerusalem."

"At the house? He came to the house?"

"Yes."

"Were you alone?"

"Yes."

"But didn't Magdalene meet him later at the tomb? That means he walked right through the city in the dead of night to your house, and after visiting you he then walked all the way back to Golgotha. Is that correct?"

"I wouldn't try to describe his movements. You see, things are different now."

"But isn't it plain that if he went to visit you in the city, and was later seen at the tomb, then he must have returned. The question, and I think it's a fair one, is *why* he went back to the tomb."

She laid down the knife and for a moment fixed her soft eyes on me. Then she turned her head and looked away. "I'm afraid you will not understand. Not yet." Her tone and the expression on her face said she wasn't trying to be mysterious, only that she preferred to drop that line of inquiry.

"Could you tell me something of the meeting itself, how your son entered, what he said. I suppose you were greatly startled to see him."

"No, not startled. I was waiting for him."

"Waiting?"

"Before he was . . ." She stopped, lowered her head, and shut her eyes. I guessed she was trying to block out the awful picture of her son on the cross. Then she looked up and resumed. "Several days before that morning at Golgotha he told me what would happen. He told me he would come back to me on Sunday morning."

"I see. I see." It was difficult to continue in the face of this sort of extravagant nonsense, especially when spoken in such a matter-of-fact way. I picked up a large red onion from the table and began peeling it, remaining silent for a minute or two. Finally I almost blurted, "But what reason could you have for believing him? I'm sorry if this is hard for you to talk about. It's just that I don't understand! Surely your son's words must have been something of a shock to you—like the raving of a condemned man. I'm sorry but I must be blunt."

"Because he told me."

"Yes, but what I'm asking is *why* you should believe what he told you. There must have been some clear reason for believing your son, something definite that made such an astonishing prediction sound plausible."

"Several things. His whole life."

"Can you tell me just one of those things? Tell me, if you will, the one most significant fact about your son that convinced you he could emerge alive from his tomb."

Hesitating, she dropped her eyes. Her manner had become almost shy. Finally, in a subdued voice she said, "I think we won't speak of this now. It's not yet the time."

A disappointment. I'd been all set to hear a long account of something rare and marvelous, complete with angels and visions and messages from on high. "But whatever it may have been, it was enough to convince you that"—here I searched for the strongest phrase I could muster—"that your son who was made like us of mortal flesh could rise from the dead?"

Readily and firmly she replied, raising her eyes to mine again, "More than enough."

The wave of curiosity that surged over me was hard to control.

What on earth could she mean? But I noticed she was becoming uncomfortable, so rather than press the question just then, I changed the subject, at the same time making an effort to curb my eagerness. "I suppose that as soon as your son left, you went to tell Peter."

"No, I stayed in my room, giving thanks."

"You didn't rush to tell the others? How could you hold yourself back?"

"It wasn't my place. Do you think Peter or anyone would have believed me? His own mother? Would you?" That charming smile again.

"What did Jesus say to you? I mean of special interest."

"I'm sorry, I must keep that private for now. I've told no one yet. I'm sorry." There was a pause, then she added almost in a murmur, as if to herself, "I may never tell."

"Of course. Beg pardon." My eyes were smarting and watering from the onion. I put it down and moved my chair back. "Your husband, I presume he is not alive or I would have heard something of him before this."

"Poor Joseph died nine years ago next month."

"Was he a fisherman?"

"A carpenter. And a very good one, too. Oh, he loved working with wood, shaping it. And he loved to talk about it. I've often heard him showing how the lines and curves of a thing could be made to follow along the natural grain of the wood. That was his favorite."

"Was he a very religious man? Would you say he had much influence on his son?"

"Joseph was deeply religious, though I think he may not have been so much concerned with all the ritual. It's hard to tell about influence. I know he and Jesus talked a lot. Mostly he was a practical man who enjoyed working hard—and he was really an excellent carpenter, the best anywhere around where we lived!"

"Did Jesus ever work at that trade?"

"Oh, yes. He was nearly as good as his father. Mostly he made tables and chairs and cupboards. People in Nazareth liked his work."

"He was born in Nazareth?"

"No. In Bethlehem."

How stupid of me! I should have anticipated that. Who didn't know the prophecy about the Messiah being born in Bethlehem? Micah, and quite clear in the text. But for some reason it had not occurred to me. Obviously it had occurred to Mary. Or Peter, more likely.

"But aren't you from Nazareth?"

She gave a light, knowing laugh, as if she'd guessed what was on my mind. "You're old enough to remember the census of Quirinius, how we all had to return to the city of our ancestry."

"Why, yes. That was, let's see, more than thirty years ago. You mean you and Joseph went back to Bethlehem for the census and Jesus was born while you were there?"

"Yes."

"Forgive me, but unless you stayed in Bethlehem many months, you must have known you were pregnant before you went. In fact, you must have been pretty near your time. I imagine the trip down there in your condition could not have been pleasant. But I suppose arrangements had been made for you at the home of some relative."

"We had no close relatives there, I mean there were some but we'd lost touch, so we didn't start the trip until almost the last minute. Jesus was born in a . . ." She hesitated, groping for a word. "I suppose you'd call it a stable, but it was made in a sort of a little cave behind an inn. With so many people on the roads, everything was so crowded we couldn't find an empty corner, much less a room. I suppose we should have expected that. Oh, Joseph was very annoyed! But I didn't mind. It was a nice stable, cozy and warm, and we were very grateful to the man who let us use it. Next day Joseph found us a room in a private home." Smiling inwardly as if fondly recalling something half forgotten, she finished, "We had a soft little manger that first night, just the right size for the baby. But we had to interrupt the poor donkey's dinner." As she finished she resumed cutting and slicing the vegetables, her head bent to her work.

I stared at her. A stable! Jesus born in a stable, a barn! And here his mother admits it, says it right out. Peter's great Messiah born into the world like any waif, born among straw and stink and filthy animals! Wait till news of this gets around. A stable!

She must be more naive than I could possibly have imagined, giving out such a story. I suppose it had to be true. Who would make it up? What advantage was there in it? Anyway, it's a safe bet that Peter will soon put a stop to her talk of stables.

"And then you came back to Nazareth?"

"No, not right away. We went down to Egypt and lived there for a while."

"Your husband's business, I suppose."

"No . . ." She'd finished preparing the vegetables and began heaping them into a large iron pot. The debris she swept off the table into a box. Moving toward the fire with the pot she went on, "The child was safer there." Stopping abruptly as if she'd made some mistake, she turned and looked down at me for a second, openly staring. Then she turned back to the fire, hung the pot and ladled in water.

Safer? What did that mean? From what?

The door opened and Salome leaned in. "Excuse me please, sir, but I must help get the dinner, if you don't mind. Everyone's staying over, and the men'll be back soon. Won't you stay and eat with us? It's mutton."

"Thank you, very kind of you, but I think not. My man is waiting for me down at the dock. I'll leave you ladies to your work." I stood up to go, then remembered another question I'd meant to ask. "Just one more thing, if I may," I said as Mary came back from the fire. "Several times I heard Jesus use the phrase, son of man. I neglected to ask him precisely who or what he meant. I know the term is used in scripture. But can you tell me his meaning exactly?"

She stopped and stood with her hand halfway toward another iron pot, the look on her face again showing a dim uncertainty. "He meant himself," she replied at last, picking up the pot. "Jesus is the Son of Man."

"Himself? . . . I see."

But I didn't see. If it was him, what did he mean about Moses lifting up the serpent in the desert? And what about the son of man being lifted up the same way? . . . no, it isn't possible. He couldn't have been predicting his own crucifixion. That was a whole year before. A striking coincidence, admittedly, but if he did mean it that way, where would the cure come in? The parallel breaks down there, and I recall him as being precise when he spoke of this sort of thing, leaving few loose ends. She's only guessing, I decided, an honest guess, of course, but it's not likely she'd have a correct explanation for every random remark made by her son.

This is no ordinary woman, I thought as I pulled shut the door of the house behind me. Given a chance to invent some spectacular tale about her son in support of all the nonsense, she draws back and declines. Then in the next instant she blandly volunteers the most damaging information! Even more impressive is her lightness of heart, so unlike the picture I had formed of a mother sunk in misery and gallantly bearing up.

Has she gone quietly mad, her mind unhinged by the sight of her boy on the cross? Deliberate falsehood seems out of the question. Either she's telling the plain truth as she understands it, or she has slipped into some sort of detached mental state where she need not face the brutal fact of her son's death. So it's the latter, I concluded, much as I dislike the idea and wish it wasn't.

Always, it's the poor mother who suffers most.

◆

JOHN'S HOUSE is a good half hour's walk from the lake shore, where I'd left Hazor waiting at the wharf with the boat. He had suggested it would be better if I went alone to question the women, and I had agreed. Now as I walked back down through the noisy streets of the village, the delicious aroma of cooking sausages filling the air, I was thinking only how good it would be to get to the inn. The headache had calmed, but now my neglected stomach was acting up, and I found myself warily considering my landlady, how I could persuade her to serve me a quick meal in silence. You'd think she never had anyone to talk to, the way she rattles on when she's able to corner me (I still hadn't met the good Jacob and I'd begun to understand why). But I didn't like to offend her.

I spotted Hazor from a distance. He was standing on the long stone wharf near its outer edge, just above where the boat was tied up. I could see that he was talking with someone, and as I came closer, with a little start I recognized Thomas the Twin. Despite my fatigue, I suddenly felt very glad to see him there, for right at that moment there was nobody I wanted to question more. He'd been in the cove that night with Peter and the others, I thought. How will he manage to explain Peter's wild story about meeting Jesus, how will he get around the necessity of calling his chief in so many words a liar? I'm afraid my greeting to him was a little abrupt.

"Well, Thomas, good to see you—and what do you think *now* of your friends' chatter about Jesus coming back from the grave?" Even as I shook his hand I couldn't help noticing how much he'd changed. There was a buoyancy to him, a freedom and a brightness in those usually wary eyes.

"What do I think! Why, only that it's all true! Yes, true! And this old world's a wonderful place!" Eagerly he reached out, put his hand on my arm and said happily, "My friend, I've been waiting here to tell you. Jesus has indeed come back from the grave, come back to us in the flesh as he was before, and the whole world will never be the same! Death couldn't hold him, Nicodemus, couldn't hold him! I want you to *know* this. I want you to *believe.* Your companion here, too."

Vividly I recalled his emphatic insistence that he would never believe unless he could examine the wounds, and I actually stammered my question: "You . . . you've met him . . . you've examined his side . . . hands . . . ?"

"Oh, I met him all right! But . . . here, let's have some privacy. Come sit in the boat and I'll explain." The three of us went down the short flight of stone stairs and stepped into the boat. I motioned Thomas to take the cushioned seat in the stern. Hazor and I sat together in the middle facing him.

"You recall that afternoon I went to your villa? Well, several days afterward Jesus came to the upper room again, and I was there. He walked right up and stopped not three feet away from me, holding out his hands. In his eyes there was the hint of a smile. Then he spoke, very calmly, and invited me to touch the wounds. As you can imagine, at first I . . . well, anyway, I finally managed to look down at his hands. The ugly red punctures were there in plain sight in the wrists, the torn flesh, the straggles of caked blood. The wound in his side was just as plain. But I didn't touch him."

"Didn't touch him! After speaking so fiercely about it? The need to verify?"

"I know, I know . . ."

"Thomas, you're not making sense. All you had to do was reach out. What stopped you?"

"I stood there transfixed, staring straight at him. There was something in his eyes, in his whole face that held me. It still bore the marks of the beating by the soldiers, especially one long ugly bruise right across from chin to brow. But from the first instant I looked at him I was certain beyond doubt who it was. It never occurred to me to touch the wounds."

"Wait, Thomas, how could you poss—"

"I was surprised at that myself, that I could be convinced by sight alone. But I hadn't changed all that much. If I may say so, I still kept hold of my natural self-possession. I was aware of myself, knew where I was, recognized my surroundings, windows, walls, tables. I was conscious of the others crowding in around us. With a feeling of settled conviction I knew that my eyes were not deceiving me, that it was indeed Jesus standing before me. I knew it just as I know that *you* are sitting *there.* Touching his wounds at that point would have been grotesque, a mere matter of curiosity. Also, there was this: would anyone but Jesus have taken such a risk, knowing all I had to do was reach out?"

"Describe that bruise across his face please."

He raised his right hand and drew his finger diagonally down his face. "A long slanting welt, puffing the left eye, the bridge of the nose, and the right cheek."

That was a precise description of the facial wound I had noted as I covered the body with the cloth. How could Thomas have known of it? He'd been nowhere near the corpse, wasn't even at Golgotha. He'd run off in fright with all the others. It must have been the women. Some of them must have had a close look when the corpse lay at the foot of the cross. They could have told the men.

"Thomas, did you know about that facial welt before? I guess it was described to you earlier, before your meeting him. That's why you felt so positive."

"No . . . I don't think so. In fact, it was seeing him like that for the first time, and so close, that made me notice. It gave me a jolt, I can tell you. Why?"

"Oh, nothing. Listen, Thomas. You say you felt no desire to examine the wounds? Well, I think that's incredible. There's simply no denying the fact that you missed your chance! You could have done so much to bring a more rational approach to all this delirium. Why couldn't you have gone that one intelligent step further?"

"Nicodemus, stop and think. If I were to tell you, here and now, that I had examined his wounds, probed them with these fingers, what would it mean? Suppose I told you that the wounds *were* real. Would you be able to accept his resurrection as a fact? Just from my testimony?"

I brushed the question aside. "That's hardly fair."

"Or would you claim that I wasn't a reliable witness, too shaken and agitated and so on, or that the wounds were faked and the man was an imposter, or that I was deluded or lying, or anything else that might bolster your doubts? You'll agree that would be the reaction of a logical mind." He emphasized the word by drawing it out—*lo-gi-cal*—and a knowing smile flickered round his mouth.

"Please go on, Thomas. What else did he say to you?"

"He spoke in a relaxed and friendly tone, and I'm sure he meant what he said as much for the others as for me. He said, you believe because you've seen me, but blessed are those who have not seen, yet believe. Those were pretty much his words."

"That sounds like a scolding to me, Thomas, a rebuke, as if he thought you were out of line for being the least bit cautious."

"No, no, Nicodemus. Remember that I was the *only* one who didn't see him the first time. You'll admit that that placed an unfair strain on me. The others saw him and I was asked to believe on *their* word, without seeing him." Wrinkles appeared at the corners of his eyes and he seemed anxious, as if he were making up his mind about something. "Being left out like that, well, I can admit now that it hurt. Me, the only one left out? *Me*? But he understood. He gave me the chance to make the test, if I wanted. What he said wasn't about my caution. He was simply *comparing* the two things, faith and proof, teaching the others as well as me. He was saying that there are times when faith is better than proof, deeper and stronger, times when faith must take the place of reason. But don't forget he *did* give me the chance."

His eyes had an inward look, as if he were sitting there alone in the boat, talking to himself. Suddenly he darted a glance from one to the other of us and said urgently, "Some things yield *only* to faith! Nicodemus—Hazor—you two still have that blessed opportunity. Seize it!"

Raw enthusiasm fired his penetrating gaze, and it all began to seem rather stupidly childish. Feeling awkward and uncomfortable, I turned away to avoid those moistly shining eyes. At the same time I inquired, as casually as I could, "Have you seen him again, I mean since that day in the upper room?"

"Yes, once, a marvelous encounter! It was a week ago. Back over near Bethsaida. We'd been out fishing all night, a few of us with Peter. We had no luck and we came in closer. There was a small cove and he was waiting for us on the beach. He stayed with . . ."

I motioned him to a stop, perhaps a little too brusquely. I'd heard enough and was in no mood to sit through another version of the tale. "Thanks, Thomas. It'll have to wait. We're late getting back and I just recalled I have some things to take care of." He got up, said a smiling good-bye to each of us, and climbed out onto the wharf. Then he turned around and gave a farewell wave, accompanied by another vigorous shout of "Seize it!"

We waved back in silence, then pushed off. For several moments Hazor sat gazing at Thomas on the wharf, then he picked up the oars and set them in the locks.

Taking short, easy pulls he kept our head parallel to the wide curve of the land, no more than about fifty yards out. A few other boats, including some larger ones with sails furled, passed us as they left the Capernaum docks or pulled in toward them. But none made any more sound than a whisper on the calm water. Though the sun was obscured, the day remained deliciously bright and warm, no wind, not even a breeze, and I soon began to feel that the whole scene spread around us—a melting combination of slate-blue sky, light blue water, blue-green shore—had a dreamlike quality to it, unreal, almost magical. It was a very pleasant sensation and lasted a long while, until Hazor broke the spell.

"What d'you think, sir, about that bruise on the face?" He had stopped rowing and was sitting there looking at me, with the oars reaching straight out on either side like wings.

I knew what he meant. I'd begun to think the same thing myself. "First you tell me. Was it the truth, that he didn't know beforehand about the facial bruise?"

"Maybe. Didn't strike me as a lie, the way he spoke, the look on his face. Seemed honest. But you know he *could* have gotten it from the women, and of course there's another way."

"Yes?"

"Well, obviously, if they stole the body."

"True. But in that case why would Thomas risk claiming to know about it if it only goes to prove that he had access to the body at some time *after* the burial? As a lie, it's worse than clumsy—and that's true even if he learned about the facial bruise from the women. He'd have guessed we'd be thinking exactly what we're thinking now."

"Right. Yet he's the one who brought it up."

At that we both fell silent and sat hunched over, staring at the water while the boat lazily turned circles. Sparkles of light twinkling off the bright, dancing surface caught and held my attention, while over me by infinite degrees there stole a most forlorn feeling of being somehow lost and alone.

I could resist no longer and I knew it.

Everything I could recall from my own personal knowledge told me that it was a dead man we carried into the tomb that day. A lifeless corpse. And yet, sitting there in the boat, recalling the earnest faces of those three women in my room, and Peter's calm assertions, and Hazor's list of names, and Thomas' glee, I felt ready to consider that we might have been wrong. When I bound those bloody wrists together and placed coins on those eyes, was it really possible that some faint embers still glowed in that great heart? Was it possible that Jesus had survived the horrid ordeal of the cross? Is that why no sign of grief marred his mother's face?

Yes, it was possible.

There! It was out! Admitted! But only to myself, my private thoughts. To Hazor I said nothing, couldn't just then, not even to save my life. Shaken right down to my sandals, I felt that just by looking at me Hazor could spot the change, as if the words were written all over my face. I lowered my head and put a hand up to my forehead to shade my eyes.

Hazor stirred and roused himself. Listlessly I watched as his arms began pumping the oars with an easy rhythm. Finally I made up my mind about our next step, and I glumly announced that it was time to go home. "Our business up here is finished, there's no more to be done. We'll pack tonight and leave for home first thing in the morning." Our next move, I added, would be made back in Jerusalem and it would take some careful planning. "We'll talk about it later."

All the way back to the inn I sat huddled on a cushion in a corner of the stern, morosely studying the luminous haze that veiled the wide lake's distant shore.

Part III

SNUG ONCE MORE in my own cozy study at the villa, sunk down on my spine in my roomy old chair, Sarah sitting opposite me so calm and looking her lovely self—that was all I needed to bring the world right side up again.

We'd been lounging and talking for a good two hours. At least I'd been talking, rattling on about what happened in Galilee. Mostly Sarah listened, now and then halting me to ask a question or get in some remark. It wasn't so much what she said. It was the way she said it, and just the fact that she was there with me. More than once I've asked myself, what is this knack she has to settle the mind and soothe the spirit? I remember how even as a young girl she always . . . but enough of that.

She did surprise me in one way. She agrees that I'm now forced at least to consider that Jesus may not have been dead when placed in the tomb. And she's not much troubled over the problem of how he could have recovered so fast. She shrugs and says who knows? Those first appearances in Jerusalem were hoaxes of some kind, she thinks, and that crowd in Galilee didn't see him until three weeks later. A strong man, she says, a man who had great powers of will like Jesus, might recover from a lot in three weeks. Enough to stand up and talk for a while.

"But, Sarah, what about the shroud? Why would Peter leave it behind? When he took the body—I suppose we can't say body anymore—why did he remove the cloth and leave it there on the stone bench? And why did he go back for it?" To me, the whole business of the cloth was not a minor matter, not incidental, but presented us with a major discrepancy.

Sarah shrugged that off, too. "Ah, Nico, who can say? Maybe a dozen reasons. Just pick one that fits. You can't know for sure, so for now you pick one. Later, when you get more information, you'll change."

It wasn't as simple as that, I told myself. It all hinged on whether Peter and his men knew what they were doing. Did they break into the tomb in order to recover a dead body? Did they go there expecting to steal a corpse, only to find him still alive? Did they somehow know that he was still alive before they broke in? It seemed to me that in each case the discarding of the burial cloth could have been done for a different reason.

"You pick one, Sarah. Let's see how it fits."

"Well . . . all right, say Jesus was still alive, but unconscious. He was naked, so Peter decided that the burial cloth wouldn't be enough to cover him. Also, if they were seen or found out on the way back it would look strange to have a man wrapped up in a shroud—to say the least! So they brought some other clothes along with them and they dressed him properly."

I tried to picture it—the Galileans stealing up to the tomb in the dead of night—taking greater pains to break into the chamber noiselessly—stopping to remove the shroud, the chin cloth, the wrist bindings—taking more time to dress the body before removing it. All this with a detachment of Roman soldiers hovering outside.

"Sorry, I can't see that as a fit."

"Nico, I think you're letting that cloth get in the way. The question is him, was he alive or dead? Alive, I should say."

"Maybe. But I just can't think why Peter and John would have gone back to the tomb to retrieve that cloth. I mean in either case. Or did they go back? If they didn't, then how did they get it? The women? But why all this lying over a simple burial garment? What's the purpose?"

"Nico! We've forgotten Joseph. Why not see what he has to say. He's old, but you know he's not easy to fool. Let's ask him over."

"I have already. He went back to Arimathea, and he's still traveling on business. I sent a note that I wanted to see him as soon as he's home. But you know as well as I do just what he'll say. He'll insist that Jesus was certainly, positively, definitely dead. You know that way of his. I can hear him rumbling at me now—'Nicodemus, you old fool, it was a corpse we put down and no mistake. *A corpse!* Everyone knows that but you. You're all tangled up with that hairsplitting again.' And what else could he think?"

A light tap sounded at the study door and the housemaid stepped in. "Sir, Hazor has arrived."

For several days I'd been eagerly awaiting Hazor's visit, and had begun to wonder what was keeping him. On the way home from Galilee the two of us had spent hours going over in detail the confused picture at the tomb that first morning when so many people had been milling in its vicinity. He'd finally agreed with me that it was time to search deeper into the whole business. (I still hadn't told him about my change of mind, however, though several times I had been on the verge.)

We'd already taken the testimony of the women. Now we needed to question the Roman guards, at least the two who'd been on duty. Vinucius had forbidden us to do that, of course, and had confined those men to barracks. But a whole month had passed. I thought we'd see what could be done now, if not directly then in some slyer way that would get round the centurion—underhanded methods, to be sure, yet at times indispensable to the business of the detector. Hazor was to take the first step, using his contacts among the large maintenance crew at the Antonia to get information on the two guards. A ticklish business, not without danger.

"Yes, good. Show him in."

Instead of Hazor it was Naomi who walked through the doorway. On her face was a mock frown, but more than half serious, and she walked straight over to me, waggling her finger. "Now, Father, you're not going to keep him talking all day. He's telling me about Galilee, especially that storm on the lake. Why didn't you say how awful it was?"

Well. Hazor and I had agreed not to mention that little incident, how close we'd come to disaster. Why cause worry? But obviously my pretty Naomi had coaxed it out of him. Hazor wasn't quite the iron man after all.

"Awful?" Sarah asked, sitting up straight. "What was awful?"

In the doorway stood Hazor, hands clasped behind his back, looking sheepish. "Sorry, sir. It's just that—"

"Never mind. Come in. Sit down. What have we got on those two guards?"

Naomi went over and took a place on the sofa. Tucking her skirt in at the side, she made a little sign for Hazor to join her. "No need to crowd," I suggested, "plenty of chairs. Here, Hazor, take this big one." Quickly he changed his direction and slid into the high-backed chair to my right. With that, Naomi turned her head and dropped her eyes in an elaborate show of unconcern, and I smiled to see the look that I'd seen so many times on her mother's face.

"What storm, Nico?"

"Just a squall on the lake one day when we got too far out by accident. Nothing much."

Naomi wouldn't let that go by. "Nothing much! Hazor told me you were both thrown out of the boat."

"Nico! Not really!"

"Well done, Hazor," I said dryly. Over his embarrassed face there spread a closemouthed grin.

"You were thrown out of the boat, Nico? But you can't swim! And at your age, too."

"What about my age? I'm not doddering. We got back into the boat. That's all. And here we are. Everything's fine."

"Father, that's not what Hazor told me. He said neither of you can remember how you got back."

"He said that, did he? Well, my young babbler, go on and tell it all. Get done with it."

Both women pushed forward and turned toward Hazor. As he talked his eyes were mostly on Naomi, and to me it seemed that he took more time and added more embellishment than was strictly required. Especially in describing the puzzling climax he didn't stint himself, making it all sound like some grand epic. On and on he went, and I was about to interrupt when Sarah broke in.

"You know, Nico, that's strange. I heard a story like that from Joanna, or maybe it was Salome. Last year, when they came up for Passover. They said the men were out on the lake fishing and a bad storm came on—just like you said, Hazor—and Jesus was there or appeared or something, and then the storm was over and the boat was safe at the shore, and no one could remember what happened. I paid no heed when they told me the story, but isn't that peculiar?"

I could see what was coming, and rather than lose another twenty minutes going over Galilean gossip, I pointedly ignored Sarah's interruption. "Very good, Hazor. Well told, if maybe a little overdone. Now, if no one objects, can we please get back to those guards?"

"But Nico, how did you and Hazor—"

"Sarah. Please? Go on, Hazor."

"But Father, doesn't it seem—"

"Please, Naomi, we'll get to it some other time. We have more important business now."

Hazor swung toward me, looking serious. "Yes, sir. We've made a start. The two guards are no longer under full restriction at the Antonia. Once a week they get passes to spend an evening at the Two Eagles. But orders have just been issued to both for a transfer. They're being sent to the Syrian Legion in Damascus. They go next Monday."

"Well, well. Getting them out of town? Or just ordinary army business? Any others going with them?"

"Don't know, sir. Got a man working on that."

"Go on."

"Names are Euganor and Calvus, both privates. Euganor is nineteen, a farm boy. Been in service two years, has eighteen more to go on his enlistment. So far, no combat. He's disgusted with army life, wants to go home. My informant says he wouldn't be surprised if the boy deserted."

He reached into his pocket, pulled out a piece of papyrus and glanced at it as he continued. "The other one, Calvus, is thirty-six, has two years of service left. Veteran of nine battles. Heavy drinker. Twice refused offers of promotion. Hates the thought of retirement, even with the land he'll get and the pension. Always saying how he wants to finish up under the sword in combat. Despises garrison duty. A rough customer."

Turning the papyrus over, he paused to look up at me. "Something else I think you'll find interesting. *Neither* of these two men served with the crowd control unit at the temple last Passover, as Vinucius claimed. My man was able to check the guards' duty roster for all those days and nights. He says Euganor and Calvus aren't listed. Either there's a mistake in the records or your brave centurion is a liar."

If so, I thought, he picked a strange thing to lie about. Was it to prove the fatigue of the guards, and excuse their sleeping on duty? Or could the lie, if it was a lie, have had a more subtle purpose—to make more convincing the very idea of one of these highly disciplined soldiers committing so serious a military crime. In this case two soldiers, and manning the same post. But that line of reasoning led in only one direction, straight to the possibility that the two guards were not asleep at all.

Sarah got up from the couch. "Come, Naomi. Time to look after dinner. I'll send in a nice drink for you two. Now, Hazor, you must visit us again soon, and not just on business."

Hazor jumped to his feet and nodded pleasantly as Sarah went past. The smile he bestowed on Naomi as she drifted after her mother was much more boyish and warm. It's a rare sight to have a capable young man turn into a calf before your eyes, and to see your own daughter, not yet sixteen, confer upon the calf in return no more than a queenly bob of the head.

◆

THE TWO EAGLES TAVERN occupies a spacious, vaulted cellar only four short blocks from the Antonia. It's a low hangout for the Roman soldiery, not the sort of establishment the council cares to have inside the city walls. But the Romans say their troops must have the place for off-duty relaxation. So they keep things reasonably quiet, the council looks the other way, and everyone pretends it's not there. Of course you still have the occasional messy street brawl when the soldiers roll home to the Antonia in the small hours. But they're soon over, thanks to the Romans' efficient Military Police.

It was in this unsavory den that we managed at last to meet and talk with young Euganor. Or I should say where Hazor talked with Euganor, for this was an outing in which I had no role. The whole idea was Hazor's. I would never have thought of it, especially the part about donning the off-duty uniform of a Roman private. This I felt was far too daring, but he insisted that with so many Roman troops stationed in and around Jerusalem, six or seven hundred, there wasn't much chance he'd be spotted. I finally gave in when he showed up at the villa one evening, stood in the center of my study and whipped off his cloak with a sweeping gesture, one arm raised in a mock pose. He was dressed in the buff-colored, knee-length tunic with the wide leather belt I'd seen a thousand times on soldiers in the city streets. Looked well in it, too.

That same evening I finally told him, still a bit reluctantly, about my change of mind concerning Jesus' survival in the tomb. He might very well be correct, was how I phrased it, in suggesting that a spark may have remained in the body, a spark later fanned to life. At this, he surprised me by saying with a careless shrug that he'd been aware of my changed view for a long time, ever since our encounter with Thomas on the Galilean shore! Smiling slyly, he said he could even pinpoint the moment when it happened: "In the boat, a few minutes after we left Thomas on the wharf. You dropped your head behind your hands. I knew that sooner or later it was bound to happen, after all we found up there, and I'd been watching for a sign."

"Yes, well, very good" was all I could answer, flustered to think I'd been so transparent. "But we still have the problem of how that half-dead body was extracted from the tomb. So if you insist on risking your neck as a spy, and since those two guards will be shipping out very shortly, I suppose you'd better get on with it."

His adventure began a few evenings later. As arranged, Hazor's informant brought us word here at the villa that Euganor and Calvus had left the Antonia. There was no problem about their destination. The six-hour pass restricted them to the Two Eagles and they had to be back in barracks by midnight. Hazor, looking very martial, left for the tavern as soon as it was dark.

As usual the Two Eagles was crowded to the doors, every table occupied, a rumbling din of talk, music, and raucous laughter filling the overheated air. Thick stone pillars every ten feet or so curved down from the low, vaulted ceiling and had the effect of dividing the large, squarish cellar into a maze of small cubicles. These ringed an open space at the center where the dancers performed to the rhythmic whine and clang and tinkle of the incessant music. The noisy relays of tawdry dancing girls added to the sense of continuous distraction. It was this loud, jumbled atmosphere that allowed Hazor to isolate his man right in the midst of the crowd and to start him talking.

With the description supplied by Hazor's informant it was easy to locate Euganor even in that mob—very young, blondish, a narrow, innocent face, and round his neck a short chain holding a bronze-and-jade talisman. Hazor, drifting unnoticed through the crush, found him sitting at a round table off to one side with five other men. All were soldiers, all were young—Hazor saw immediately that the older Calvus was not among them—and all were well along in their merriment. Euganor, while not acting drunk, still appeared less than sober.

Sipping a drink, for a while Hazor lounged against the wall nearby, listening to the talk at the table and laughing along when a guffaw went up, even throwing in a few sallies of his own. When one of the young merrymakers invited him to sit down, he wedged a chair in next to Euganor. Soon the two were talking, their exchanges lost in the general uproar.

In friendly fashion, Euganor inquired where Hazor was from, of course meaning the hometown. But Hazor alertly took advantage of the opening. "Damascus. The Syrian Legion. Reassigned here a couple of weeks ago. Signal Corps."

"Hey, I'm getting transferred up there myself pretty soon. What's it like?"

"Not bad. Not so strict. More things to do than down here, that's for sure. You'll like it. Except for the guard duty. Out on the frontier mostly, not in the city. I heard we pull a *lot* of guard time down here."

"Not all that much, mostly in the city. One tour a month maybe, sometimes two, depends."

"Not bad, I guess. Hey, is it true what I heard, that we had to guard a *tomb* a few weeks ago? Was it really a tomb? Man, that's crazy!"

Euganor grinned. "Yeah, we did."

"I heard a couple of the guards were caught taking a snooze. Never happen in Damascus—up there, just one time and you're gone, you know? You don't get a second chance." Hazor drew a finger across his throat as he spoke, then he fell silent and turned away to watch the three wildly gyrating dancers then on the floor—better slow down, he thought, don't press, give the young man time to react.

The music wailed and moaned, driving the three whirling women and their flying veils faster and faster. Very deliberately Euganor raised his tankard and took a long drink. "I had that duty," he said in a subdued voice as he put the tankard down. "I wasn't asleep." Then, brightening, he asked, "Hey, what about the girls up there?"

"Great! Friendly, too, not like these Jew girls down here, won't even smile or say hello when you meet them in the street. Say, if you weren't asleep, what's all this stuff I hear in the barracks, the body's missing or something?"

"Centurion says we can't talk about it."

"Why not? Man, it sounds weird!"

"Dunno. Aw, who cares anyway. All them Jews are tricky, ya know? Tricky. But what I can't figure is how they done it, that funny light."

The high-pitched music swelled piercingly, reverberating off the stone pillars and the bare walls while the dancers leaped and swirled, filmy costumes flowing, anklets clinking, clinking. Hazor kept still and let his gaze drift around the crowded room. Euganor took a drink, then wiped his lips with the back of his hand as he leaned over and whispered, "You ever have night duty in a graveyard?"

"Nope."

"This was a graveyard. Bunch of tombs all around. Man, I don't like graveyards. I mean I heard some stories."

"Yeah."

"And it was dark, lemme tell you! Couldn't see nothing from where I was, just the campfire off under the trees. Spooky. Everybody sleeping 'cept me and Cal."

"What d'ya mean the Jews are tricky?"

"Not supposed to talk . . . but I mean I don't see how they done it . . . how they got the body out."

"There was a light?"

"Yeah. And you know what? The ground shook. I mean it *shook*. Right under my feet. Then the light showed."

"You scared?"

"Naw. Well, I guess a little. I mean that light was scary, just sorta seeped out around the edges of the big stone. Bluish, kinda, then yellow. Suddenly it was like the whole stone was blazing, the whole thing. Not on fire, wasn't no red like in a real fire. The stone just lit up bright, blue and yellow. Blinded me, sorta."

"What'd you do?"

"Ran and woke up the centurion, me and Cal."

"What'd he do?"

"When we got back there was only a sort of a glow. The centurion told us to move the stone away, open the tomb. He was real excited, boy was he excited."

"Yeah, so?"

"We couldn't, not right away. Me and Cal and another man, we took hold, but the stone was hot, and it felt, I don't know, tingly I guess, something like that. I yanked off the sealing cord and burned my fingers some. Had to wait a while before we could get a grip."

"You go inside?"

"The centurion went in. We waited."

"How come?"

"He said so. After a while he came out and told us the body was gone. But I mean how could it? We were right there all night, me and Cal and the others."

"When you ran for the centurion how long did it take to get there, rouse him and get back to the tomb? Try to be precise." No sooner was the question out of his mouth than Hazor realized he had made a mistake, stepping out of character and sounding more like an official inquisitor than an enlisted man. Euganor, for all his slow-witted air, caught the alteration in manner. "Huh? What difference does that make?" he asked, turning to look directly at Hazor.

Giving an elaborate shrug, Hazor twisted his head away to watch the dancers. "So all right, so you can't talk about it. So forget it," he muttered unconcernedly, as he motioned to the waitress threading her way between the tables. "Let's have another drink. I gotta get back soon."

There was another few seconds' pause, with Hazor holding his breath, his face averted. Then Euganor went on. "Gee, I dunno. Not long. First I got ahold of Cal, then we went and woke the centurion and he came pretty quick. I guess—"

From nowhere a huge hand swung down and thumped resoundingly on Euganor's back, shoving him violently against the table. Hazor's nerves, keyed up all evening, leaped in panic, and he flung around in his chair, ready for trouble. From the description he'd been given he quickly recognized the veteran Calvus, a large, balding, black-bearded, mean-looking individual. But Calvus was showing broken teeth in a broad, crooked smile, and he was quite drunk.

"Here y'are, young pup!" he boomed thickly. "Come on, I got a sojer's drink for you, not that dishwater." He grabbed Euganor under one arm and pulled him roughly to his feet. Giving a low raucous laugh, he began dragging him away, ignoring the struggling youth's good-natured protests.

After they'd gone only a few feet Calvus stopped suddenly, then turned round and glanced back inquiringly at Hazor. "Who's your ugly friend?" he asked Euganor. "Never seen him before."

"New man, Cal. From the Legion in Damascus."

"Yeah? I got friends up there. When'd he get in? I thought Damascus was short-handed. Hey, new man, you know anybody up there in the Fourth Invincibles?"

The expression on Calvus' face seemed a shade calculating, and for a split second Hazor hesitated, wondering if there really was a unit of the famous Fourth Invincibles in Damascus. Then casually he shook his head, "Nope."

"What outfit?"

"Uh . . . headquarters."

"Legion or cohort?"

"Legion."

For a long moment Calvus stared, then he rasped, "Some soft duty," and abruptly turned away, yanking at Euganor. But Euganor hung back. "Wait a minute, Cal, he can tell us about—"

"Hell, I ain't got time to hear about no Damascus. We still got a whole lotta drinkin' to do, and they's only two hours left." Throwing a final inquisitive glance back at Hazor, Calvus pulled the complaining Euganor after him and the two quickly melted into the boisterous crowd.

◆

AFTER LEAVING THE TWO EAGLES, Hazor came straight back here to the villa, and we sat up practically all night talking and making notes, wrestling with the implications of this new evidence—and soon had to admit that we had too many fresh angles to allow easy conclusions. Immediately obvious, of course, was the fact that the women's testimony about their part that morning could be taken as completely reliable. No wonder they didn't see any of the guards. They'd all gone. No wonder the young man in white was able to wander about so freely. No guards to stop him. Or I should say the two young men in white.

One fact, we agreed, was inescapable. Things couldn't have happened exactly as Euganor said, for that would mean Jesus had vanished out of a sealed chamber. So Euganor had definitely left something out, or else there was a good deal he didn't know—which brought us to the mysterious blaze of light.

Interpreting Euganor's unfinished statement, from start to fade-out the light flash didn't last very long, four or five minutes at most, with the tomb left unguarded for about half that time. Could the theft could have been managed in such a brief span, and in those tight circumstances? Hazor's own experiment, he reminded me, had proved that the removal could be done in less than two minutes. "The light flash may have been set off as a diversion," he suggested, then added doubtfully, "but how was it rigged up inside the closed chamber? If they did get the body out, how did they avoid the six guards, who must have scoured the area?"

There were some real problems with the theory, yet we agreed that in a case like this everything had to be looked at, no matter how improbable. "If they didn't take the body in those few minutes while Euganor and Calvus were back at the centurion's tent," Hazor asked, his brow knitting in perplexity, "when *did* they get hold of it?"

For both of us the sticking point was that sudden great flare inside the tomb. The cause of the phenomenon, whatever it was, must have been remarkably powerful. I had heard of some fairly strange things happening to stone, in volcanic action for one, but I could recall nothing that explained this eruption of light in what amounted to an underground vault.

Such a blast of illumination must have come from the burning of fuel suddenly set alight—wood or rushes or charcoal or pitch, or some kind of oil, or resins or gums, or better, some combination of all these. Hazor mentioned the stuff they call nephthar, which in fact may be likeliest, a thick, dark liquid that burns fiercely, even erupts in the presence of fire, they say. Nephthar or not, whatever was used here, there must have been a lot of it. This we stated for the sake of argument, since neither of us was sure that the burning of any amount of fuel could have given the spectacular effect reported by Euganor.

In this regard our most pressing questions concerned the actions of Vinucius. Did he find any remains of fuels in the chamber, unburned residue? Was there any sign of how they were gotten in, how they were disposed, how they were set alight? A charred container, or its ashes? Blackened earth or walls? If he did see something, why were there no traces of it later when I got there?

Of course, it would be easy to decide that the flare was just something imagined or exaggerated by a frightened young rustic trembling alone in a burial ground. But Euganor's description was fairly detailed, even noticing the peculiar coloring of the flame—if it was a flame. What sort of fire burns without red? Might be something there. And what about the strange condition of the stone when he touched it: hot and tingly.

Then there was that troublesome sealing cord across the stone. Was it possible that the cord was tampered with earlier, loosened somehow, so it could be quickly replaced? But if, as Euganor said, the guards were there all night and not distracted or sleeping or something, what then?

It was no use, we admitted at last. There were simply too many pieces that didn't fit, no matter how we moved them around. Finally, at dawn we gave up and I sent Hazor home in a carriage to get some well-earned rest. Before he went I made sure to congratulate him on his night's work. My admiration for him had never been higher than at that moment, and I had to ask myself how much longer he'd be content to serve as my administrator. Such cool daring and quick intelligence, it was plain to see, marked him for bigger things.

Two days later, two long, frustrating days, after I had again gone over and over Euganor's information, the only result was that my aching brain was in a permanent whirl, a loose wheel on an overturned cart spinning helplessly. Probably I would have gone on like that, getting more and more tangled and depressed, if young Mark had not come in to break the spell with his exciting news.

But the events of this day, the fortieth since our investigation began, were crucial, and deserve careful recording. I'll only state that I have added nothing to what actually happened, and, to the best of my recollection, have left nothing out.

◆

A*S THE MAID ANNOUNCED* the boy Mark, he scooted past her, tripping on the rug and almost falling in his haste. Then he ignored my greeting as he blurted, "Peter says if you wanna meet

Jesus you should go to Olivet right away!"

"Peter says what? Take a breath, boy! Say it again."

He gulped twice, then repeated, "If you wanna meet Jesus go to Mount Olivet—they're leaving the house right away and going there—you should go there too Peter says."

"Are you sure, boy? Isn't Peter in Galilee? He told you that himself?" My heart had begun a thumping that I thought must be audible in the next room.

"They came back—he told me to run—I ran all the way."

I shouted for the maid. When she didn't appear I went to the study door and bellowed even louder. From around a corner in the hallway she scurried into view, her eyes wide. "Tell them to get my carriage ready. With a driver. Have it at the front in three minutes!"

I raced back through the study, down the rear hall, and up the stairs into my bedroom, where I threw off the old dressing gown I was wearing. Grabbing the first pieces of clothing I could find I hurried into them. Then I stopped and hovered nervously in the center of the floor trying to think if there was anything else I should do. There wasn't. Out through the door I dashed again and went rapidly down the main stairs, my breath coming heavily.

The carriage was just rolling up to the front door, hitched to the big pony, the fast one. I had my foot on the sill ready to climb in when, looking up, I was startled to see Naomi come running into the yard through the outer portal. She was shouting and waving her arms, her long hair tangled in the wind.

"Father! Wait!"

I hastened round the carriage to meet her. She ran up and flung herself at me, crying out in a strangled little voice, "Father, they've arrested Hazor!"

"Arrested? Who has?"

"The Romans."

"What for?"

"I don't know, I don't know! I went to the north grove to see him and the men said he'd been taken away a few minutes before."

"Where was he taken?"

"The Antonia. We have to go there. Get in the carriage. Oh, Father, hurry!"

"Listen, Naomi. I don't know what's going on, but you know it can't be anything serious. If they took Hazor in a short time ago, then he'll be all right for a while. Look, dear, I'd go with you this minute only I've just had a message that Jesus . . ."

Not waiting for me to finish, she turned and climbed into the carriage behind the driver. I reached up and took her hand. "Peter sent word that Jesus will be at Olivet. Hazor will be safe for an hour or so. I'm sure of it. We'll go to the Antonia right after Olivet. Only an hour."

"No, no, Father, you can't go to Olivet. You can't! Not now. Later you can go, but those Romans, you know what they're—"

"Naomi, you know that if I had the slightest thought that he was in any real danger . . . only an hour?"

Tears had begun streaming down her cheeks. "Oh, Father, if anything happened to him I couldn't live!"

I suppose I knew from the first what the outcome would be. I will say that there was one desperate moment when I felt ready to turn the girl over to the servants and ride off. Now, faced squarely with Naomi's distress, I began to wonder if Hazor actually could be in danger. Was the arrest linked to that evening in the Two Eagles? Had that brute Calvus sniffed out something and reported it? Impersonating a Roman soldier was a dangerous thing to do, especially in this city. Spying would be the least of the charges.

There was only one way to find out. But even as I climbed in beside Naomi and ordered the driver to make as fast as possible for the Antonia, I was calculating how long it might take to reach the fortress, arrange Hazor's release, and then get to Olivet. Fortunately, the Antonia lay in the same direction as the Mount, in fact more than halfway.

I'd forgotten something—that maddening city traffic.

As the carriage turned hastily from the villa into the street, we found the way blocked by a lumbering, overloaded wagon moving at a snail's pace. Fuming, we inched along behind it until the street widened. Three blocks farther on we were again slowed by a bunch of idiotic goats dashing out from a narrow alley and milling around in fright ahead of us, all bleating in protest as we pushed through.

In the main thoroughfare we had to give way again, this time for a long procession of schoolchildren straggling past us in giggly pairs. I could hardly keep myself from jumping down from the carriage and running the whole distance.

Beside me, Naomi sat fidgeting with her hands, and I was sure she'd burst out in tears again when, as we swung on two wheels round a corner, we smacked hard against the side of another carriage. The metal wheelhubs crashed resoundingly, sending out a shower of bright sparks. Somehow the iron-rimmed wheels locked hard, so we had to get down to lighten the load and wait while a noisy crowd gathered. The two drivers, once they had done shouting at each other, began to tug and lift.

By the time we were freed and everyone had calmed down we'd lost a good twenty minutes. Then we were off again, and when we finally pulled to a halt in front of the broad steps leading up to the Antonia, at least a half hour had passed since we'd left the villa. As I got out Naomi made a move to follow, but I said that no daughter of mine would set foot in a Roman barracks. Firmly I ordered her to stay in the carriage and I instructed the driver to keep her there. Rather than waste time, she gave in.

The man on duty at the desk, after checking the roster in front of him, readily answered my question. "He was brought in a couple of hours ago. No charge yet."

"On whose orders?"

"Centurion Vinucius."

"Please tell the centurion that Councillor Nicodemus is here and would like to see him."

"He's barracks officer today. Says he won't take civilian business. Come back tomorrow."

"Please tell him I'm here. I must see him today. If he needs a reason, you can say this to him—the tomb seal. Tell him I want to talk about the tomb seal at Golgotha?"

"The tomb seal at Golgotha? What's that?"

"Just say it."

The man shrugged, then pointed to the waiting room, the same one I'd talked to Vinucius in before. I walked over to it and entered, closed the door, and sat down at the middle of the heavy table in one of the stiff-backed chairs. Leaning back, I took a long, deep breath and let it out slowly.

The fat's in the fire now, I thought.

Muffled footsteps approached rapidly to the door. Abruptly it was thrown open wide and Vinucius, resplendent in full uniform, filled the entrance. The crested helmet, the shining breastplate, the dark red cape hanging to his knees, all made him seem huge and gave him the typical Roman air of command. But as I looked at the cold, hard face I spotted something else. In those deep-set eyes I was surprised to detect a tinge of apprehension.

He came in without speaking and closed the door. Removing his helmet he placed it at one end of the table, then went around to the other side and took a seat. He still said nothing, only stared across at me, that sharp and knowing stare. But this silent inspection didn't fool me any longer. It was his usual try at intimidation, gaining the upper hand before anything was said—they must all learn it at some officer's training school, I concluded. Interesting that when you know about it the little trick loses its power, even becomes a bit laughable. But I didn't laugh.

Coolly I returned his stare, almost enjoying myself, determined to make him ask the first question. He was evidently too anxious to play the game for long, for I could tell from his drawn look that he was going to speak even before he opened his mouth.

"What is this about a tomb seal?"

"What is this about my man Hazor?"

"Your man?"

"He's my overseer. You didn't know?" I smiled.

"Whoever he is, he's in for questioning."

"Concerning what?"

"Tampering with a tomb."

"And just what does that mean?"

"Explain about the seal."

"We'll get to the seal. I'm here to declare that Hazor has done nothing wrong, broken no law. I'll vouch for him and I want him released immediately, if you please."

"Nothing? My report says that he spent a whole night fiddling with something at the Galilean's tomb several weeks ago. That case's still open, you know."

Vinucius had no idea how relieved I was to hear him say that. At least it wasn't a spy charge. "Then you have nothing to hold him for. What he did at the tomb that night was by my direction. I demand his immediate release."

"You'll demand nothing!" His fist banged down on the table and my heart skipped a beat as he thrust his head across toward me, his lean, young face blackening into rage. But once again I recognized the calculated nature of his anger. Outwardly calm, I went on.

"Hazor's business at the tomb that night was not illegal. By my orders he was trying to determine how the body might have been taken. You recall my first visit here? You recall I asked how that big stone could have been moved without waking you? There are ways, you said. I was trying to find a way. That puts us on your side, doesn't it, the side of the law?"

Glowering, he leaned back in his chair, obviously unconvinced. I took a breath, said a silent prayer. then plunged on, ready to follow wherever instinct took me.

"But our little experiment at the tomb was a waste of time, wasn't it? Tell me, Centurion, how do *you* think the body was removed so handily from that guarded chamber? And by the way, I suppose you've heard the talk—it seems that the Galilean wasn't quite dead after all. Not quite. It looks like your executioners bungled the job this time."

He waved his hand impatiently. "I've heard the stupid rumors. But he was dead. Good and dead. I guarantee it. What about that seal?"

Something in his assured, offhand way of speaking, something in that brief and casual "I guarantee it," brought me up short. The absolute last thing I wanted to hear was someone claiming to offer proof that Jesus had definitely died on the cross. I didn't want to allow myself even to think of it as a remote possibility.

"How can you guarantee it?"

"You think any man could have survived what we gave this one?

You think we're amateurs at this business? We don't certify a criminal as dead until we *know* he's dead. Anyway, I went in and checked the body for myself the day we set up. Dead. And later when I heard the talk I spoke with Centurion Longinus. He agrees there's no chance the man was still alive, not a chance. Our army physician pronounced him dead, you know. A smart old man and he followed the regular procedure. And Pilate didn't release the body until he made sure he had a conclusive report from Longinus in person. Pilate's nobody's fool."

"I didn't see the physician. When did he—"

"Right when the body was taken down, on the ground at the foot of the cross, as he's supposed to. No pulse, no breath, no heartbeat, glazed eyes, all the rest of it. Everything according to the book, mirror to the lips, ear on the chest, everything. Crucifixion is old stuff to us, routine. We set out to kill a man, we kill him. It isn't hard to do, take my word. The Galilean was dead, and that's that."

My thoughts were suddenly in a jumble, and I found it hard to keep my mind on the business I had come for. Jesus dead? Something in my own memory of handling the corpse, the witness of my own eyes and hands, quietly insisted that Vinucius was right—the official procedures, the skill of the executioners, really did amount to a guarantee of death. And the centurion's personal report to Pilate seemed to clinch it. Almost frantically I tried to smother the thought, to shake it off, but it kept escaping, whispering . . . Jesus was dead . . . Jesus was dead . . . Jesus was dead . . .

Vinucius eyed me curiously. My shattered mood, I realized, must be written all over my face, plain to see. That could be dangerous here in this room, fencing with the lying Roman. A change in the atmosphere was urgent, so I pushed my chair back and stood up. In what I hoped was a relaxed manner I took a few steps along the side of the table, hands clasped behind my back. When I had my expression under control I turned back again and looked steadily down at my opponent.

I was ready for the final thrust.

"All right, Vinucius, you want to know about the seal. Well, it's come to my attention—never mind how—that your description of the way the Galilean's body disappeared from the tomb is not entirely correct. In fact, it is decidedly *in*correct, if that is the right word to cover what I mean."

He didn't move, didn't even blink. I remained equally still and waited a few seconds, looking straight at him. Then in a slow, deliberate manner I took hold of my chair, placed it directly opposite him, and sat down again. One after the other I put both elbows on the table and clasped my hands. "Vinucius, would you care to tell me what you saw in the tomb when you went in alone after your men reported that mysterious blaze of light?"

He didn't stir a hairsbreadth.

"Vinucius, my friend, let's be sensible. You realize how unpleasant things will get if I report the truth and how you covered it up? First, we'll have a fine old uproar in council—Joseph and I and some others who still favor truth will see to that. These things have a way of blowing up, you know, so the disturbance will get pretty ugly, then will spread outdoors. You know about Pilate. Not a patient man, is he? Hates to be bothered by little things like riots in the street.'

I paused to let the picture of a mounting street disturbance sink in, something that the disciplined Romans especially hate. Then I went on. "A simple, everyday assignment to guard a tomb, Pilate will say. And look what it's come to! He'll want to know the name of the centurion in charge. Replacing an army officer is no problem. Ship him out to some lonely frontier town, an easy way to pacify those Jew fanatics."

I had him. I could see it in the tightening muscles of his lean jaw, in the taut lips. And he knew that I knew it, I could see that too. "Vinucius, my friend, you know that I'm not bound to make such a report. As a councillor I can decide what's important. Some truthful answers from you might convince me that there's no need for any of this to go beyond these walls."

He sat there, his lean face impassive, betraying no thought or emotion. Then, very slowly, his right hand began to move, reaching over across his chest armor, the fingers stretching toward the thick, black handle of the short sword hanging on his left hip. Deliberately he drew the sword from its scabbard, inch by gleaming inch. As the broad, two-edged blade came free, he held it before his face, point uppermost. Eyes still glowering, with his thumb he tried the razor edge—then abruptly he rose to his feet, in the same motion violently shoving the chair backward with his legs.

Grasping the sword as if it were a dagger, he hesitated a fraction of a second, then suddenly raised his arm high as he lunged across the narrow table.

Panic gripped me, and while every nerve in my body jerked alive, I couldn't move. In horror, I saw the muscular arm begin its swift descent. Involuntarily I shut my eyes, at the same time weakly lifting both hands above my head in a helpless attempt to ward off the blow. There was a dull *chunk*, and then only silence. Slowly my eyes came open, my heart pounding as I brought my trembling arms down.

In the middle of the table the sword quivered upright on its point. It had been driven deep into the wood, fully two or three inches. On the other side of the table Vinucius loomed menacingly tall, fists planted on hips and his elbows held wide under the flaring red cape. In the sneering gaze he fixed on me there burned intense anger and even hatred. When he spoke, the tone of the metallic voice was harder than ever.

"You're a damned coward, Nicodemus! And you're a fool! But even cowards must value their lives. This city has so many dark alleys—have you forgotten? And there are all those deserted stretches outside the walls. Anything can happen out there to a traveler, roaming bandits . . ." He trailed to a halt but his eyes continued to bore into mine.

It's amazing how ugly and threatening the naked blade of a Roman sword can be up close. My stomach turned queasy as I looked at it, the thick, black handle still slightly swaying. But that one wild, hopeless moment of panic had already passed. As I sat there waiting for my heartbeat to slow, I was pleasantly surprised to note how remarkably calm I'd become in my mind. The explosive demonstration was another of his calculated efforts to cow me.

"Put your shiny toy away, Vinucius. To silence me you'll have to kill me right now, here in this room. But that would be very awkward and inconvenient. How would you explain it to the council, to Pilate?" He stood there in silence and it took me a moment to realize from the change that spread over his face that he was actually paying attention to what I was saying. "And if you're thinking of detaining me, forget it. I have two companions waiting outside. Unless I join them shortly they'll report my detention to the full council."

His reaction was astonishing in its lightning change of mood. Without so much as another word, almost nonchalantly, he reached over, grasped the sword and yanked it out of the table. Expertly he dropped the blade back into its scabbard, then reached behind him to retrieve the chair, and sat down. Rubbing his eyes with both hands as if he'd just awakened from a refreshing sleep, he asked, "Do I have your word as a councillor of Israel?" His tone was quite businesslike, no sulking, no resentment.

"Yes."

"Who's that god of yours? Swear on his name."

"I so swear. Now tell me, what did you see when you went into the tomb that night?"

"Nothing special. Does that disappoint you? Well, it's the truth and you can believe me. Nothing special at all."

"But the body was gone?'

"Yes."

"When you ordered the stone to be moved, I understand that the seal was still in place. How could the body have been taken without breaking the seal?"

"Some kind of Jewish trick, must have been. I looked around pretty carefully, especially at the back of the chamber, while I was inside. Thought there might be a hidden exit. There wasn't, at least I found none. But why ask me? Sorcery is nothing new to you people. Trickery's your middle name." A disagreeable sneering smile came over his face as he finished.

"Could the sealing cord and the stone have been tampered with previously, say in the time between your setting up guard the day before and the moment you yourself entered the chamber? There was an interval of about fourteen hours."

"Not a chance."

"Why?"

"Don't be stupid. We were there all the time."

"But suppose the guards on an earlier shift fell asleep? Before midnight, say. Someone might have broken in and taken the body then, replacing stone and seal so the break wasn't noticed."

"There was only one earlier night watch. The off-duty men were still awake for most of it, talking at the fire. When I made my last rounds it was almost midnight. Nothing out of place. And you can stop talking about the men sleeping on duty. Doesn't happen in *my* command!"

"What caused that light flash?"

"More Jewish trickery. Anyway, I saw it only as it was fading."

"No sign of burnt fuel in the chamber?"

"There was nothing in the chamber, just the cloth."

I wasn't surprised. I'd been waiting for this. "You mean the burial shroud?"

"What else?"

"Describe the cloth, please, how it was lying."

"It was just as I'd seen it the day before except the body was gone. Stretched out on the stone bench, head to foot. Struck me it must have been straightened up after the body was taken, neatly put back."

"How was the top half lying?"

"Stretched out too. The whole thing was stretched out, upper half covering the bottom half."

"You're sure? Could the top half have been disturbed, thrown up at the head somehow, and you didn't notice?" At my interview with the women, Hannah had been definite about that.

He was bristling again. "Don't press me, Councillor. Observation is part of my business. In that situation, a missing body, you think I'd make a mistake? Anyway, I remember that the two cords round the outside were still in place, lying across the cloth."

Until that instant I'd forgotten about the thin cords I had used to hold the shroud on the body. "Both of them still *across* the cloth? Not thrown aside?"

"You don't hear well? Yes, across. Now get on with it. I don't have all day."

"One cord at the waist and one down at the feet?"

"Yes, about."

"All right. Then what?"

"I left. Went outside to question the two guards who'd been on that watch."

"How long were you inside? You're positive you're not overlooking something? I want to hear everything you saw or did, no matter how small."

"A few minutes. Five maybe. Well, one thing. As I was leaving I noticed some low bulges under the cloth, so I picked up the top half and—"

"Of course! It was you."

"What?"

"It was you who threw up the top half."

"What are you getting at?" He looked doubtful, as if he was afraid I might pull some trick from my sleeve.

"Nothing, nothing at all. What was underneath?"

"The two small cloths, the ones used to bind up the chin and fasten the wrists. What'd you expect?"

"Where were they? Tell me exactly where and how those cloth bindings were arranged as they lay on the bottom half of the shroud."

"What difference does that make? I think you're losing your grip, Councillor."

"I'd like an answer, please."

"Well, there was the chin cloth. That was up at the top, at the head, lying flat. Still had that rounded shape. And there was the wrist cloth, farther down, about where the hands had been. Both cloths were still tied."

"Tied?"

"Knotted. Of course a chin cloth can be pulled off from around the head. But how do you take a wrist binding off without untying or cutting it?"

"Did you touch the two small cloths?"

"Picked them up to have a look."

"What did you do with them?"

"Threw them down somewhere. At the back, I think."

"Did you roll them, fold them together?"

"Might have."

He stood up suddenly and reached for his helmet. "I guess you've run out of questions if you're down to trivial stuff like that. Anyway, there's no more to tell. As I said before, it was a very clean job." He pulled the helmet on, carefully adjusting it. "You should've been a Roman, Councillor. You're wasted here." He hitched up his sword belt and gave the shoulder of his cape a tug. "What I've told you is the truth. Can't see what good it'll do you. How the body of that Galilean was taken is something I've wondered about. But I don't lose sleep over it. There's an answer. Someone'll find it."

At the door he stopped and turned for a last remark, his tone sounding almost friendly. "Keep your word, Councillor, and I'm sure we'll both live long and happy lives. And when I'm a prefect somewhere—far from this insane country—none of this will matter. By then who'll care? Wait here and I'll have your man sent up to you."

He swung toward the door, and again he stopped. This time he spoke without turning, but half looking back over his shoulder. "It was that kid Euganor, wasn't it?"

I didn't hurry my reply. "Vinucius, you had six men with you that night. By now the whole barracks must know what happened. Anyway, we'll make that a part of our deal, too. You don't even try to find out. Otherwise some stray information could still reach Pilate. Not much, just enough to raise doubts about your handling of the assignment."

He pulled himself up straight, squared his shoulders, adjusted his helmet again, yanked the door open wide, and strode out. As the trailing edge of his flaring cape disappeared around the doorway I recalled another item about the burial I'd forgotten—those two bronze coins we'd laid on the closed eyes. They'd never turned up and Vinucius hadn't mentioned them, though he'd been very detailed and precise about everything else.

Well, well, I thought as I listened to his footsteps fading across the flagstones of the central hall. You may go far in the world, my ambitious friend, but that magnificent uniform covers a very small soul.

◆

URGED BY THE REPEATED CRACK of the driver's flailing whip, the pony quickly lengthened its stride and we were soon flying along the Bethany road at a breakneck pace, just outside the city walls. At the grinding clatter of our approach the few people and vehicles strung out ahead of us moved hastily aside, heads swiveling as we thundered past, some shouting angrily.

The careening speed of the carriage was wildly exhilarating. It was also frightening. So it wasn't until we swung east, rounding into that last broad stretch to Olivet, that I was able to regain some presence of mind and to gather my thoughts. As I did so, the shock I felt can only be described as devastating.

I was now totally convinced that my own first impression had been correct, that the man I helped bury had indeed been dead. Not half dead, not almost dead. A lifeless corpse. What Vinucius told me had simply clinched the feeling I'd had in my bones all along, that nagging belief I had managed to suppress but which had never really let go. Now in my heart I had not the least doubt of it—Jesus was dead as he lay in the tomb.

And yet! Here I was risking my neck and the necks of my daughter, my friend, and my driver in a whirlwind dash in a flimsy carriage hoping to see and talk to that same man alive. Alive! The stark contradiction finally hit me with its full, naked force, and the impact of it was almost physical, like walking smack against the thin edge of an open door in the dark.

How could I hold both ideas? I couldn't, no one could, no one short of a miserable, ignorant peasant or savage. A civilized mind, a rational mind, must reject one or the other. I was not suffering a mental lapse or a delusion. I knew where I was, what I was. Around me lay the same familiar world. Yet in this one mortal instant, racing toward Olivet, I seemed actually to find myself almost on the verge of believing the unbelievable. All my careful knowledge of human weakness and human error and silly superstition, where was it now? Shouldn't I be laughing, a loud, scornful laugh? Shouldn't my reason rebel at the very thought, cry out in horror no! no! no! . . .

"Easy, boy, easy." The driver's insistent voice, gentling the snorting pony as it was reined in, brought me back. With the pony slowed to a trot, we went along another short stretch of road, and then we jerked to a halt at the start of the footpath leading up to Olivet's summit. Hazor jumped down and gave Naomi a hand. I climbed off on the other side, urging the two to hurry.

At a rapid pace Hazor and Naomi took the long, undulating slope up the hill through the trees, with me doing my best behind them. Wisps of gray-white cloud floated around us as we ascended, and I could see that, farther on up, the mist accumulated into a thicker blanket of white. The day had been dismally gray to start with, rain threatening since early morning, low clouds hanging like spumy veils over the city and the countryside. Now the dulled sun must have begun to burn its way through, for as we neared the broad, mist-shrouded top, the haze that enveloped us began to brighten.

While we were still some distance off we saw them, a scattering of men and women, twenty or so. Partially obscured by the glowing fog, they were spread around the grassy field at the summit, standing together by twos and threes. Still and silent, they all faced in toward each other forming a loose ring, some with heads lowered, a few with faces eerily transfixed. Hesitantly, a bit awkwardly, we walked among them. There was no reaction, not even a nod of welcome.

At last I spotted Peter standing by himself, huge hands clasped at his brawny chest, head down. I motioned to Naomi and Hazor and we went over to him.

"Peter, am I too late?"

Slowly his head came up, slowly his eyes lifted to mine. But he made no reply, just stared at me with a peculiar shining vacancy that was startling when I recalled my last sight of that strong face.

"Peter?"

He didn't wake suddenly from his reverie. With what seemed a tremendous effort, he lifted one hand, placed it heavily on my shoulder and said, "Hello, my friend." His voice sounded unnaturally flat.

"Peter, am I too late? Has Jesus been here?"

"Yes, he was here. I sent for you."

"I tried to come . . . never mind, I'll tell you later. Peter, what did he say, where'd he go? He can't be far . . ."

"Nicodemus, wait . . . I'm sorry you were delayed. Jesus was here with us a good while, but he has—well, he has gone—departed, and he . . . look, my friend, this is not the place for explanations, and I need some time . . . we must go back now. But you come see us in a few days, will you?"

"Yes, yes, I will. But Peter! I've obtained a confession about what really happened at the tomb that night! And I owe you an apology."

"Who's confessed?"

"The centurion. Vinucius."

"Oh." He didn't appear quite interested. "You can tell us about it when you come over."

"Peter, I do regret having suspected you. And I'm truly sorry for talking to you the way I did that first time. It was the cloth, I mean the burial shroud. It was your having it in your possession just then that made me—"

"Never mind about that, Nicodemus," he cut me off, then added with a slight chuckle, "You know, when I thought about it later I had to admit that, in your place, I believe I'd have been suspicious too! Well, good-bye for now, my friend."

He turned away and was about to walk off, when he stopped and swung back as if he'd forgotten something. "We're keeping the cloth, by the way. His blood's on it, you know, the precious blood he shed for us, for everyone—for *you.* I'm grateful that you stopped Rhoda from washing it! But we'll have time to talk of all that when you come over."

Roused by the sound of our voices, all the others had begun to move, gathering in around us. Peter reached out and gave my arm a squeeze, then threw a smiling wave at Hazor and Naomi. Turning away, he walked toward the footpath, a shambling, exhausted walk. After him straggled the whole group.

Only then, as I watched the band moving noiselessly like wraiths through the swirling mist, did I fully understand that I had been talking all the while as if the dead Jesus really had been present only minutes before! Suddenly I wanted more than anything to ask Peter as a reasonable man how he could expect me to believe such a thing without actually seeing Jesus. If so many others had seen him, ordinary people, including those hundreds in Galilee, why should I be left out—especially after all I'd done this past month to earn the privilege. I raised a hand and was about to shout after Peter to wait, when a voice spoke softly just behind my ear, making my nerves, now wound up tight, jump wildly.

"Nicodemus, my friend," said the voice, "you mustn't feel sad that you missed him."

I looked around to see Thomas the Twin standing at my elbow and smiling encouragingly. "Don't be sad, be happy. Remember?"

I nodded and smiled back. "I remember, Thomas, I remember very well. Still, I wish I'd been here to see him. I really wish I could have seen him." He smiled broadly again and said that he understood my feelings, but his advice was that I should try to be patient. Then he said good-bye and hurried after the others.

Very quickly the wide hilltop was deserted, except for the three of us. I didn't feel ready to leave just yet, needing some breathing space for my nerves to settle, so I asked Hazor to take Naomi back to the carriage and wait for me. "Yes, sir. No hurry." I watched as the two walked off down the path arm in arm (Sarah was right, they did look good together). Then I was alone.

Aimlessly I strolled around the grassy summit, trying to shake off the tension. The wind had picked up some, making a start at clearing off the heavy fog, and the breeze felt wonderfully soothing. Gradually I became calmer and finally I sat down on a big boulder in among the large clump of trees off to the side A short rest, I told myself, and then I'd go.

Too much excitement will catch up with a man, and it happens quicker when the resilience of youth is gone. I'd been sitting there on the rock only a few minutes when it caught up with me. Without warning, the whole weight of frustration that had been piling up over the past month toppled down on me. My shoulders sagged as if under a physical burden and I sat there slumped over, feeling lost and unutterably weary. What good had it done, I asked myself bitterly, all this frantic scrambling?

Was I the only one left in this entire city who cared for truth, the only one who cared enough to put aside personal affairs including business and go chasing off in search of it? Why hadn't some of the others come forward to help, men of influence, and for that matter why did Joseph choose that precise moment to go running back to Arimathea? What was so important back home it couldn't wait, when so much was going on right here under his nose? You'd think he might have felt some responsibility, some loyalty, but no, I was left alone. And really, in a few years when all is said and done, will any of this about Jesus really matter, after we who knew him and heard him teach are all gone?

I heard my name called out softly. "Nicodemus," the voice said in a low tone, sounding near and yet strangely distant. Startled, I swung round. Anxiously my eyes darted from side to side, probing among the shadowy trees. All the others had gone, I knew, and I was sure I was alone on that windy summit.

Then I saw it, farther off, a tall white figure brightly veiled in the hovering white mist, moving toward me. Unsteadily I put a hand on the rock and pushed myself to my feet, then stood there waiting, peering, my mind a churning mixture of fear and hope and doubt. Its pace measured, its movements deliberate, the shrouded figure walked steadily through the thinning fog, white garments shining in the slant rays of the brightening sun.

All my weariness melted suddenly away and my heart lifted into a thrilling buoyancy such as I have seldom known. Scarcely realizing what I was doing, with hands reaching out, I lurched forward eagerly.

"What's the matter, Nicodemus? Are you all right? You look as if you'd seen a ghost."

The speaker stood within ten feet of me, but it was some seconds before my mind focused on reality and I was able to recognize him. "Thomas," I said faintly, "I thought you . . ."

"Are you all right? You're very pale. Here, sit down."

Guided by Thomas, I backed toward the boulder and slumped down again, grateful to have something solid under me. "I thought you went away with the others."

"I did. Then I realized I might have given you a wrong impression, so I came back."

"Wrong impression?"

"What I said about being patient."

"Yes?"

"I wouldn't want you to misunderstand, to think I meant be patient and you'd get to see Jesus. Did you think that?"

"I suppose I did."

"There, I knew it! I'm sorry, it was very clumsy of me. But no, I didn't mean that exactly. Not as we have. The truth is that Jesus has left us. That's what I came back to say. Jesus has returned to his Father. He's no longer here, not clothed in ordinary flesh. But of course he's still present among us, and someday . . ."

When I'm overtired I can be pretty rude—crusty, Sarah calls it by way of softening the effect. I'm afraid this was one of those moments. "Thomas, what in blazes are you talking about! I'm in no mood for this kind of gibbering. You're a man of intellect, not a loose-brained fanatic. Make sense! Returned to his father?"

"In heaven. To the Father who sent him. Oh, but he hasn't abandoned us! He'll be with us always, his flesh and blood, to the end of time, and—"

"I see, I see. Jesus is in heaven with his father, only he's *not* in heaven. He's still here with us, only he's *not* here. Is that it?" Halfway through the sentence I regretted the sarcasm, but I'd spoken too quickly and he couldn't have missed it. I was prepared for a reprimand.

Instead, across that narrow face there broke an unaccustomed smile. "Well, I see Peter was correct, as usual. This is certainly not the moment. I apologize for pressing you. Now if you're all right I'll go on and catch up with the others. We'll see you in a few days, don't forget. Then we can talk."

I was contrite and I made a deliberate effort to let him see it. "Thanks for coming back, Thomas. It was good of you, even if we don't speak the same language." He laughed lightly, then turned with a wave of his hand and hurried off. I kept my seat on the rock and gazed after him in some puzzlement as he walked briskly across the summit, gradually disappearing down the pathway on the other side. When I recalled how fiercely he spoke at our first meeting against his friends, this change in his outlook, in his grasp of things, made no sense. And yet in a way the sheer honesty of it, the absolute, firm conviction, was compelling, even attractive.

I almost envied him for it.

As if in sympathy with my weariness, and my despondent mood, there came a sudden strong rush of wind sighing and murmuring through the trees and blowing across the open ground, lifting and tossing my hair and ruffling my clothes. I caught my billowing robe and pulled it tighter. It was time to go. The best place for me now was that roomy old chair in my cozy study, and Sarah sitting opposite. I got up, and had just begun walking when, as if in answer to a question, I distinctly heard the words, *because my reason knows that this is not a matter of reason. . . .*

Drifting across my mind like one of those lone, bright clouds that float above the darkening edge of an evening horizon, the thought grew clearer and brighter as I walked. Had I heard the words spoken? Had they been whispered on the breeze? I halted and glanced quickly around to make sure I was alone. The fog had almost lifted, blown away, and the deserted hilltop lay open to the sun.

Aloud I repeated the words: "Reason knows—it is not—a matter of reason." Nothing quite like that thought had ever occurred to me before, or if it had I couldn't recall it. Again I spoke aloud, hands held wide in an unthinking gesture of appeal: "Not a matter of reason?" Anxiously my eyes trailed around the circumference of the hill, moving deliberately from tree to tree as if I expected one of them to step forward and reply. Swaying slightly, I stood there with the moaning wind sweeping across the summit, blowing hard against me, tugging, gusting fitfully.

One flashing moment later, though I hadn't moved an inch from where I was standing, I began to feel as if I *had* moved, as if I'd run up and leaped across a wide, deep chasm. I could even feel the lingering effects of the exertion, a slight dizziness, heavier breathing. Raising a hand to my forehead to steady myself I was surprised to find it drenched in sweat.

My reason had *not* gone astray! So far as it was able, it had actually done its proper work. Along two separate pathways it had led me unerringly to two distinct conclusions. Jesus had died and been buried, that was one conclusion. Jesus had later been seen alive, that was another.

Two conclusions, two facts for me inescapable. But there—*there*—reason recoiled, faltered, fell powerless. Though my two undoubted facts concerned the same man, reason was helpless to make them converge. Then in a single dizzying instant, impelled by a force beyond logic, a truth above knowledge, they *had* converged . . . coalesced . . . entwined . . . is there a word to describe it?

God in his mercy, I told myself, for his own mysterious purpose has chosen to set aside the world's harsh verdict. To this man Jesus, this obscure prophet so cruelly cut off in his prime, he has granted a truly marvelous dispensation. When was it heard of before! He has called him out of the grave and given him a second life. Think of it—a second life! I said the words aloud, "A second life. Jesus *did* die. And he *is* alive."

The burial chamber, the shroud, the sealed stone—what of them? Once restored, how did he escape his awful prison? If he vanished from the sight of his companions at Emmaus, could he not disappear from the enveloping cloths? If the solid walls of the upper room failed to keep him out, should the obstructing stone keep him in? As he put aside the bindings and the shroud without disturbing them, so he shrugged off the tomb!

May not God accomplish such things if he wishes? Shall we here and now, frail inhabitants of this little space of time, presume to know everything in heaven and earth? Is nothing to be left for finding out hereafter?

Naomi! I'd completely forgotten about the two of them waiting patiently down there in the carriage. But being together like that I'm sure they don't mind waiting! How astonished they'll look when I tell them! Of course Hazor will be polite, won't say in so many words that I've gone soft in the head. But I wonder on which side he'll come down. Will he say that Jesus never died, or will he say that he never rose? He'll have to choose one or the other. We had some interesting evenings ahead of us, Hazor and I.

Grateful for the moist touch of the cooling breeze on my face, feeling rested and at peace with myself after many days—can it really be only a few weeks since that first morning?—I walked slowly across the grassy summit to the pathway and started down.

But how ironic! In solving the puzzle of the empty tomb I have only succeeded in burdening myself with a second mystery. And who will deny that it clamors for a solution as loudly as the first?

Just who was this man Jesus?

Or rather who *is* he?

No ordinary man, certainly, but exactly *who*?

I see I shall have to begin my search all over again. And this time, please God, I'll not be so sure of myself. The question is where to start? Peter, I suppose. Or perhaps I'll have another talk with Mary herself. I could ask Sarah to come with me.

Yes, that's it, we'll go and have a talk with his mother. She might tell Sarah things she wouldn't tell me. Sarah's good like that.